ALWAYS MINE

A Devil's Shadow Novel

Estella Oscura

Contents

Warning

This book is a dark romance book and contains many dark elements. Below is a list of trigger warnings or content warnings that you will find. If you have any issues with the following, it is recommended that you do not read the book.

Assault

Blood

Bondage

Cheating

Confinement

Cults

Death

Demons

Gore

Graphic Death

Hostages

Kidnapping

Mentions of Rape (Nothing else but the word)

Murder

Occult

Pain

Satan/ the devil

Sexual assault

Sexually explicit scenes

Stalking

Torture

Violence

Playlist

SECULAR HAZE by Ghost

Aventine by Agnes Obel

Sweet Creature by Harry Styles

Death Knell by Ghost

Love Will Tear Us Apart by Joy Division

Dead of Night by Orville Peck

Fire Meet Gasoline by Sia

Helter Skelter by The Beatles

Love You to Death by Type O Negative

For those wanting a
book with murder, sex
and possessive demons

This book is for you

Presents
under a
BIG tent!

The
Crimson Carnival
Welcomes You!

666 LIVE D. ROAD

THIS WEEKEND ONLY!

CLOSES
AT
SUNSET

ALL
NEW
ACTS

Knife Throwing!
WORLD'S DEADLIEST SHOT
Daredevil

the crimson carnival

11 YEARS AGO (BACK THEN)

GROWING UP IN A family of serial killers is easier than people think. Everything is already decided for me.

My school.

My job.

And tonight, my husband. Hopefully.

All I have to worry about is staying alive and not getting caught.

Recently, my training has been focused on knife work. That includes learning to fight with and against different blades, slicing different meats and organs with various sharp tools, and very soon cutting up a body to properly dispose of it.

I tug on the pink sleeves of my undershirt to cover up the myriad of healing cuts and stab wounds on my arms.

Okay, well, maybe not that soon.

I huff out a breath as I stare out the tinted windows. We have been in the car for almost two hours, but we are almost there. The atmosphere is unchanged, but that is the norm for us.

My gaze shoots to my older brother, who sits next to me in the back seat. At fourteen years old, he sits comfortably in his seat despite his body going through some changes. His jaw is now more defined, his voice deepening. He has gotten taller and muscles bulkier. Yet, he is still at ease in his skin. You'd hardly notice he was going through puberty.

His eyes slide my way, and he quirks a brow at me.

What? The subtle gesture asks me.

I grin at him in response, and a small laugh escapes him, making my grin grow wider.

"Anna. Mason. Keep it down back there," our father scolds. His voice is monotone, the deep tenor reverberating in the small space, but we don't need him to raise his voice or ask us twice.

We immediately go back to sitting at attention, facing forward. In the rearview mirror, my father's steely gray eyes watch us. A hint of a warning in them.

The first part of training as a child is to get rid of fear. So while I don't necessarily fear my parents, I understand how much of my life is controlled by them and how bad it would be for me to upset them.

As one can imagine, serial killers have little to no emotions and show even less. Well, most of them. I feel different in that sense- always having trouble controlling myself or letting my feelings get the better of me.

I'm told Mason was able to master the skill at six years old, while I still struggle at the age of ten. Putting me at a disadvantage, because most of my training starts with learning this one skill. It's why I'm just now going to my first carnival at such a late age.

A clear mind is a sharp mind- your greatest tool. This mantra I've heard so many times, I've already lost count. I am aware I'm the black sheep of my family, but that's okay. Even if I don't exactly fit in here, I know I don't fit in anywhere else.

Other kids my age are really something else. I've seen them laughing and playing without a care in the world. At this age, they are learning to read and maybe learning how to do division. Stuff that I learned by the age of four.

Me?

I study people's body language for hours on end, learning how to read between the lines in a conversation and how to get myself out of being caught in a lie. These practical skills are much more useful in my family's line of work. No time for fun and games. Only meticulous drills to ingrain this knowledge into every cell of my body.

I can smell the change in our surroundings a moment before the sedan pulls onto a bumpy road. The faint smell of dirt, popcorn, fried food and greasy metal filters into the car. The transition from the paved highway to the worn dirt path jostles me from my thoughts. Even though I try to keep my composure, my excitement mingles with my nerves. I feel my stomach doing somersaults as my hands get clammy.

A temporary panic seizes me. If mother or father were to grab my hand and feel the sweat, I would not get to eat for the next few days. Mason sometimes sneaks me food, but the hunger pains were almost made worse for it. At such a big event, I'm sure the punishment would be greater.

My eyes go out of focus as I gaze off into the distance and begin listing off constellations alphabetically. I fill my head with thoughts of the vast starry sky with its diamond eyes shining down, giving me a small escape and comfort. By the time we pull to a complete stop, I am at Circinus and am left with a practiced calm.

I blink and quickly take in my surroundings. We are one of many similar-looking cars parked in front of a chain-link fence. A few other people get out of their vehicles, but I don't move. Waiting for my father's signal, we get out of the car simultaneously, and I take my place next to mother while Mason hurries to stand by our father. I feel her cool, steady hand on my shoulder as she guides us forward.

Up ahead is a break in the fence with a giant white and black sign with red, bold letters reading "The Crimson Carnival". We walk through the entrance in unison, and

I fight the urge to let a shiver go down my spine. I wouldn't dare. Not with my mother's hand on me. It's not from the dreary late February evening, but from the other thing I know is waiting for me.

A faint mumbling can be heard up ahead, and we quietly walk past the empty rides and booths, straight towards the giant red and black tent in the middle of the empty circus. Before we make it to the entrance, my mother's hand tightens on my shoulder ever so slightly, and I pause to look back at her.

Her eyes quickly scan over me in my black velvet dress before she reaches to the top of my head and straightens my matching black bow. When she's done, I look up at my father and see his stern approval before he nods at mother. She opens up her bag and brings out four painted masks.

I reach out for mine, and a swell of pride goes through me. I might have missed out on being here a few years earlier, but I am here now and ready to make my family proud.

Looking down at the white, smooth jester mask in my hands, I admire the craftsmanship. Perfect symmetrical blue hearts on the cheeks with intricate gold designs outline the eyes. The coif adorning the top of the mask is also blue and gold, ending with silent bells.

With the mask securely on my face, the world appears through two small holes. It's a calculated risk losing so much of our vision, but we know in the tent we are not allowed to fight or kill once we are on these grounds. A designated safe zone. Even so, I finger the twin blades in my pockets and let the smile hiding behind the mask free.

We turn to the tent again and walk forward as a unit. I make sure my breaths stay even and controlled as we step through the entrance of the vinyl tent and towards what my future holds.

an angry heart

Blood rolls down, dripping onto the cement floor. The steady *plop, plop* of it as it pools under the man who is currently hanging on meat hooks from my ceiling. The holes the metal created in the soft flesh of his shoulders only gives some solace to my demon.

The metallic scent of blood laced with the sweat from fear and pain is like a balm for my angry heart. I am always angry when I am away from her, but there are rules to follow and a job to do.

Soft guttural whimpers escape his throat as the hooks continue to tear through the tendons and muscles. I missed his lungs, but only just barely. I didn't actually want him to die.

Not yet.

The sound of my feet echoes back to me as I walk away from the bloody mess of a man, wiping my hands as I go back to my tool table to pick out another fun toy and return my used ones. The sconces on the wall in my vault flicker with flames as they cast shadows in the dark, damp room.

The man's name is Greg Little, and he is a trained serial killer. A killer who decided to stray away from the traditions he is meant to follow. So here he hangs now, facing punishment.

To him and the rest of my flock, I am the judge, jury, and executioner. My word and rule are absolute. Should anyone dare to go against me, they will find themselves either dead or in Greg's position, just depending on my temperament.

Unfortunately for Greg, he caught me in a bad mood. The last two months have been nothing but meetings and monitoring rituals- this time of the year being busier than normal for me.

It is getting more painful as the days stretch into another week. My body and heart scream at me to return to the dark-haired woman who owns me wholly. We just have a little bit longer to go. For now, we will just take pleasure in making others suffer with us.

Behind me, I hear Greg's breath hitch as he comes to. I give him a few more minutes to fully awaken before we get started again. We are at the tipping point where his unconscious periods will last longer than his conscious ones. The exhaustion from the prolonged pain finally catching up to him.

Luckily for me, it usually takes a while to get to this point, thanks to the training my little killers go through at a young age.

The first thing they learn after reading, math and other basics is how to control their emotions. Unnecessary, overly emotional ones are cut from the flesh, then we beat the fear and aversion to pain out of them until they are numb to both. Until they show us nothing and otherwise become nothing.

Then comes basic athletic skills and manipulation of the mind. Learning what different tools you can use for killing and dismembering. It's a necessity to be able to use what can be found around you to get out of any situation you may find yourself in as well as learning how to take pride and enjoyment in your work.

All of our kills look like what people would call "freak accidents". Never anything that would draw too much attention to them, therefore us. It's how we have continued for so long. This is a way to express their artistic skills and show off what each of them can do. As long as you don't get greedy, don't stay to watch and keep things clean, my people are free to develop whatever trademarks and figure out what prey they like to hunt.

This is how everyone stays safe and keeps my protection. They think we keep them safe from just human law alone, but they have no idea what the true demons would sell for a chance at their tainted souls. Because of me and my family, they can focus on what is really important- worshipping us and growing our followers.

Power from their devotion is how we remain powerful. Fear of what they cannot see, yet they continue to have blind faith that we are doing our job. That's what keeps me strong. Humans aren't able to see me unless I want to be seen. They actually don't want to see me. My presence is a death sentence. A curse. It foretells an unfortunate ending for you.

There is only one girl who has ever seen me and interacted with me. A human girl who is now grown up. Her seeing me didn't end in physical pain, but the damage that was done from it spread between us both. It is a pain that is branded on my soul just as she is. Even if I want to, I'll never forget.

Greg's raspy breaths turn to moans as he fully wakes up.

"Please, please, please, please…" he begs repeatedly.

I turn to face him, and I tsk. "You should know better than to beg."

His head seems to hang lower with my admonishing. "I'll do better. I was being selfish and stupid, but I know better," he rasps, still a desperate plea.

"Hm. I know you'll do better," I mutter.

Turning back to my tools, I pick out the black jagged blade. It's shorter than a machete but bigger than a butcher's knife. The jagged edges are all different and gnarly in appearance. It was made from Periayer- a cursed metal mined deep from the depths of Hell. I pick it up and watch the dark metal glint in the dim lighting.

"M-m-my l-lord?"

"There's not much that is asked of you. Not really when you compare to what is given. The rules are so simple to follow: learn the ways, attend the meetings, stick to the rules- don't get greedy and, above all else, don't kill other Shadow members. Yet, someone got greedy, didn't they?" I purr.

Greg says nothing, but his breaths come quicker as he begins to hyperventilate. His eyes trained on the blade in my hand.

I move closer to him until I can smell a mixture of his sweat, urine, and blood that permeates the space.

"Do you know what's so special about this blade?" I whisper.

He shakes his head no, wincing as the movement causes the hooks to dig further into his back.

"This blade doesn't just cut the flesh." I run the tip of the blade around to the back of his tricep. I apply pressure until I feel it push into the soft skin. He lets out a low grunt, but I keep going, sawing the skin and muscle away from the bone with the jagged knife ever so slowly. Blood splatters over me and him before a steady stream forms and begins pooling at my feet, joining the rest of the drying blood puddle.

When I'm halfway up the muscle, he finally lets out a terrible scream. His body shakes from the pain, his face pales, and a cold sweat breaks out over his clammy skin. I don't stop though. I happily continue until the muscle is cut messily from the bone.

The freed flesh drops, and with a sickening splat, lands right into the bloody puddle. Greg and I both get splashed by the puddle that he hovers over. He is no longer screaming. Only weak, mournful wails fall from his bruised and cut lips.

"Now, the great thing about this blade is that it cuts not only your physical body, but deep into your soul. Every time I cut off a piece of you, a piece of your soul gets cut away as well." I flash him an evil grin. "Now let's see how much more of you I can cut away before I stitch you up and send you back to the herd as the little obedient sheep you are."

twenty-nine murders

PRESENT DAY

THE BITING CHILL OF the night seeps through my sweater as my nimble body hugs the brick wall. My eyes are trained on my target ahead of me as I watch forty-eight-year-old construction worker Robert F. Gilles finish his frozen to table dinner and start washing dishes. His routine never changes. I should know. I've been watching him for weeks now.

I'm at the point where I have to fight my urges to get my favorite curved knife and butcher the fucker right now. He deserves it. Oh boy, he sure does deserve my blade shredding through his muscular, taught abs, making the dedication to attain such a physique pointless.

Why is such a fate given to the worm? Because Robert F. Gilles is a rapist.

The justice system is a joke. This pathetic man has gotten away with not just one, but eleven counts of varying assaults, including sexual assault and forcible rape. And what has happened to him? He got three hundred hours of community service. Barely a slap on his wrist, but what a slap in the face to his victims.

I remember the boiling rage I felt when the pig caught my attention and then the immediate feeling of pure delight as the lucky bastard not only made my list, but put himself at the very top of it.

Oh, how sweet it'll feel to make *him* the victim one fateful day. How absolutely divine it'll be to see the terror in his eyes the moment he realizes his last moments of life will be controlled by me. What a wondrous occasion to celebrate, for women everywhere knowing there's one less pathetic excuse in the world to worry about.

My cheeks burn and I realize I'm grinning. I quickly drop my smile and try my best to clear my thoughts, but it doesn't work. After a minute or so, I sigh and decide to call it a night.

I shuffle quietly from the ledge I am perched on when a strong gust of wind causes me tighten my grip on the dark brick. The roof I am currently on is a thirty-story building, and it goes without saying that the fall would be less than ideal. After the wind dies down, I continue forward until my feet return to the solid roof.

Suddenly, a familiar prickle breaks out along the back of my neck, but before I can sink into the sensation, a blossom of unease spreads through my chest. I spin slowly, my eyes scanning my surroundings, but I already know that I won't find anyone there. Just an empty roof. Just like always.

Quickly gathering my belongings, I take my leave and head back home.

NOT SURPRISINGLY, I'M THE first one home. It's a little past midnight, and my parents are still on their own hunts. Mason left the house years ago after he got married to the Glippe's middle daughter. So I am all alone, but it isn't all bad. Especially when I have the house to myself like this.

I head to the kitchen to whip up something quick for me to take upstairs. I am going to miss doing this- used to the routine I've had for years. Killers are creatures of habit. The idea of change is less than off-putting, but this is tradition and I couldn't stop it.

I finish up, head upstairs, and, since my hands are full, nudge my door open with my boot. Once inside, a smile spreads wide across my face, and I let out an exaggerated yawn. I set my food on my desk before stripping down until I'm just in my underwear and tank top.

This is the only place I can ever be myself. My safe place. It is better with an empty house because when I know others are here, I still have to dampen myself to an extent.

This is what I live for, but I know no one else can see this side of me. The side that allows me to express myself beyond blinking and talking. It is a hidden moment of paradise, but my days enjoying such freedoms are numbered.

My twenty-first birthday is soon, too soon. My coming of age means my marriage to Theodore Henry follows close behind. Teddy is three years older than me, but we had to wait. Our code requires the youngest partner to be at least twenty-one before the couple can marry.

Teddy is okay. He doesn't talk to me much beyond what is necessary. We have been betrothed for eleven years now, and while he wasn't too excited when we were first chosen for each other, he has been decent enough after our continued interactions.

I know his parents are some of the good ones, and that he is an only child. My parents tell me he is a fine choice, and that I am lucky he was chosen for me.

What do I think? I don't know. When I think of him, I am conflicted. Part of me is excited for my life with him, but the other is not fully convinced he's the right choice. It makes me think I'm maybe just excited about the thought of him and not him as a person.

He grew up to be much bigger than me, but then again, at five foot four inches, most people are. He's handsome too, which is never a bad thing. I'm the most nervous about finding out his signature and who he goes after. Those are intimate details you can only share with your spouse, not a peep before you're married. While we do know our community individually, that information is to be kept hidden unless it's someone you really trust.

For example, everyone in my family knows each other's type, but only because our parents were the ones who taught us and trained with us. I know my mother goes after abusive men who beat their wives, my father goes after the same—a total coincidence and something I'm told doesn't happen often. My brother goes after child predators and, well, I go after people who the justice system failed to punish.

I'm told it's unique, not having a more specific taste. In the Devil's Shadow Society, we are taught to trust our instincts and do what feels right. To me, there's nothing that feels more right than delivering my own justice, and with twenty-nine murders, I'm hoping I can complete number thirty before the end of the month. Then I'll be ready to marry Theodore and become Anna Henry. Perfect wife and serial killer.

a matched pair

Back Then

I sit in front of my father as we wait for the meeting to begin. We are on an elevated balcony he conjured up for us to watch the masked killers entering below. All of them don unique masks to their family line, something that makes them identifiable while keeping their faces hidden.

My father, Azrael, and I can see right through them. We know who everyone is. One of the many powers we share as demons. He lounges his large body comfortably in the oversized seat. His makeshift throne, nothing like the one we had back home, but it does fine since this is a traveling circus, after all. Nothing of permanence here.

At least that's what it's supposed to appear like.

Azrael has been over the society for decades. I was created to be next in line to take over. Just like his father before him and his before him and so on. This isn't anything new, just simply the way of our race. I was born with knowledge passed down from long-lived generations before me.

My job is to watch over our worshippers and remind those who stray from our flock why they should never turn their backs on The Society. Today there will be a pairing, so our presence is required to bless the pending union. The time has come for a girl who is finally of age to choose her future mate.

Daughters are rare in this line of work, so most of the time when the males age out, it's on them to create a perfect wife with the woman their parents choose for them. In previous years, that hasn't been much of an issue, but it looks like with this generation, that will be the case.

The stands are filled with what looks like a couple hundred in attendance. A buzzing sensation starts low in my spine as the human leader stands up in front of the large crowd and begins the meeting with some prayers and chants in reverence for the Balor demon family- my family. While we do have a natural amount of power that thrums through us, it's the worshipping that really fuels us and keeps us strong.

After almost an hour into the meeting, it is finally time for the match to be made. A girl with a jester mask stands up from the Wilson family. She has long dark curly hair, half pinned up in a big bow, and a black dress with a long-sleeve pink shirt she tugs on.

That's all anyone can see from the outside at least, but not me. With my abilities, I can see more than that. Like her big green eyes that are wide with eagerness. The fact that she is biting the inside of her lip to fight back a smile, and the faint blush that taints her tanned olive cheeks.

Behind the mask, she is free with her expressions because she thinks nobody can see, but I see it all. A grunt from my father lets me know he can also see it. I watch the girl and catch her eyes flicking up to where we sit and widening.

My heart stutters in my chest.

There's no way she can see us. Is there? Nobody should be able to see us. We are invisible to humans, and I've never heard of a case where anyone has seen through the barrier unless we will it. Her smile stretches before she looks back towards the line of boys in front of her.

I risk a glance towards my father and catch his steely gray eyes on me.

"Is there a problem, Ciarán?" His deep voice rumbles.

"No," I answer, keeping my face and voice devoid of emotion.

He stares at me a beat longer before nodding and turning his attention back to the ceremony in front of us.

The girl has already washed her hands in the ceremonial oils and has a knife poised over her tiny tanned hand as she slices it open. Dark red blossoms over the cut, but she doesn't make a sound or flinch. Her eyes stay focused on the blood welling in her upturned hand as the speaker puts the crystal in her palm and wraps her fingers around it.

A strong wave of power hits me, and I suck in a breath before I ball my hands into fists. My skin ripples slightly, and I am immediately put on edge as the full icy gaze of Azrael Balor is upon me. I don't dare move a muscle as I fight against the urge to change into my demon form.

My nails dig further into my skin as I breathe through my nostrils until I have control over myself. I know it's been a while since a mating match has occurred, but I don't remember having such a strong reaction before. Maybe now that my powers have grown, this is more normal. I'll have to remember that for next time so I can be better prepared.

The boys follow suit and cut their hands, letting their blood flow freely. They range in age from six to twenty, all of them eligible and still looking for their mates. With the crystal coated in her blood, her lively green eyes glance up at me quickly before she paints a smirk on her face and takes a pass in front of the line of young men with all their hands out towards her.

Her hand grips the chain secured to the crystal as she methodically makes her way down the line. Her steps are light as she stares straight ahead. When she gets to the end, she pauses before turning around, going back the way she came. One by one, the males pull their hands back as their blood sizzles, showing their incompatibility.

There are three boys left standing in the line. Those who struck out are now kneeling with their heads bowed. A few of them I can see are biting back their pain behind their masks. Either her blood is very strong or this generation of killers needs more training. I am going to have to keep a closer eye on my flock.

At last, there is only one boy left. As the girl walks past me to him, the crystal hums.

Another intense wave of power spreads through my veins, and I squeeze my hands tighter as my eyes follow her. She hesitates a moment before she gets to him, but as she does, the crystal shatters. The crowd erupts in hushed whispers before the speaker rushes over to her. After a few moments of their heads being bowed, they straighten up, and the speaker announces them a match.

The girl is Anna Wilson, and the boy is Theodore Henry. He is my age and the only child in the Henry family. The followers clap their approval, but my eyes stay on Anna as her face twists into a frown behind her mask. The couple walk outside for privacy, as the tradition states for them to remain outside for the rest of the meeting so that they may get to know each other better.

I relax a little and look down at my fists. I unclench them, staring at my open palms. My nails had broken through the skin and are now sticky with my black blood.

playing normal

PRESENT DAY

"LATTE READY FOR CHARLOTTE!" Jen announces to the busy café. It is midmorning on a Friday, and work is in full swing.

I have been working at Lots of Lattes for years now, and I worked my way up to the manager's position. Management has pushed me multiple times to move up positions in the local chain, but I don't want that. This is the furthest I can go on the totem pole without having to put any more effort in. Either way, working here is a front.

What really demands my attention is my hunt, my kills. Money is important, sure. But the devil we worship always provides, and I need to make sure I am doing my part to give back to him.

Today is the last day of training for our latest new hire, Penny. I have trained so many people over the years that I could do it with hardly any effort. She will be picking up the slack while I am gone, since I am about to get married and be spending weeks on end with Teddy.

Coincidentally, my last day will be today for the next month. I have my assistant managers who will cover for me. Plus, I never take off anyway, and they always tell me I should.

I do like it here. I can act more naturally in my own skin and interact with people in a way I can't in my home life. Laughing at jokes, staying busy and keeping track of the store is very fulfilling for me. While I can see myself doing great things if I took the district manager position, I am happy where I'm at. Even if I can feel I am missing something.

Nothing beats the feeling of true satisfaction of watching blood pour out of a wound caused by your own hand. By seeing the final look of terror in another's eyes as they realize you are the one in control in this moment. Their last thoughts will be of you and the pain that you caused. That is what I truly love.

Still, sometimes it feels like something is missing. Like maybe someone to share the high after my kills. Someone to have a connection with or would understand and know me better than anyone else. That's what I was promised to have with Teddy, but sometimes it feels like he hates me.

"Anna, your fiancé is here!" Jen calls to me.

Speaking of the devil.

We are supposed to meet up regularly leading up to our marriage, but Teddy never lets me visit him. He insists on coming to me. It is a nice gesture, and even though he seems happy to see me- well, for the most part- there is always something that feels off with him. It is questionable why I am not allowed to go with him, but he is firm in telling me no, and I have learned to just drop the subject.

"Going on break! Penny, you okay to handle the machines alone?"

"Yes! I'm pretty sure I've got it," her bubbly reply follows.

"Okay, be back in half an hour."

With that, I slip off my apron and put it away before walking over to where Teddy waits for me by the door.

He has an easy smile curving his lips today and holds his hand out to me. I take it, and his hand tightens around mine before he pulls me forward. The bell chimes on the door as he opens it and leads us onto the sidewalk.

"Hi Teddy. What are we doing today?"

"How hungry are you?" he asks.

This is more than just a simple question. This is a test.

Starting a couple of years ago, he asked me the same question. He had been taking us to nearby places to eat, but soon we ran out of things to talk about and started just sitting in silence. It had been okay. It reminded me of home, so I was used to it.

One day, he asked me the question, and I admitted I wasn't so hungry. He then surprised me by taking me to a nearby secluded area, and we had sex for the first time.

He said, since we are going to be together, that it was okay. I had never heard any rules against it. It was fun, and he was good at it, I guess. It was definitely better than the silent meals we had, that's for sure.

He seemed satisfied enough and taught me how to please him, and, in turn, he did the same for me. It came as a close second to killing, that was for sure.

We've regularly met and experimented with what he likes, but even then, I still feel our connection is missing something. I wonder if he feels the same, because it has been a while since he asked me that question. Honestly, I haven't even missed him. Is that normal? I guess serial killers really aren't attached to anything or anyone.

Not wanting to talk, I am about to respond that I am not at all hungry. But my body betrays me, and my stomach lets out a loud growl. My face heats, and Teddy's grip on my hand tightens, causing me to look up at him. Before he can smarten his features, a look of pure anger pierces me.

Startled, I jump back and yank my hand that's in his grip, but he doesn't let go. I glance down for a second to see his knuckles turn white from the grip he has on me.

When I look back up at his handsome face, I see the emotionless stare of a Shadow member. Of a well-trained killer.

"Teddy…"

"It's fine, Anna," he says in a monotone voice. He doesn't yell, but I still feel the full sting of his words as if he had. "I don't want to hear it."

But it isn't fine. I know he hates when I show any emotions. He really just hates knowing I am human at all.

His bruising grip on my hand doesn't let up as he silently pulls me along to the closest restaurant, and I follow behind, stifling my sigh.

I can never do anything right with him.

Come on, Trouble

BACK THEN

I EXCUSE MYSELF FROM my father's presence as the meeting continues on. His gaze is penetrating, but he does nothing to stop me from leaving.

Heading outside, I move in no particular direction, yet I know where I'm heading all the same. I slow my approach as the sound of awkward conversation reaches my ears. I get within a few feet of the pair, and even though I know they shouldn't be able to see me, I still hide behind a ticket booth.

"My name is Anna," a voice as sweet as honey says. "I'm going to be your wife."

"I guess. My name is Theodore, but you can call me Teddy," an awkward, deeper voice says. The voice grates on my nerves, and I ball my fists in response.

"Oh, a nickname! I love nicknames. I've never had one. My name is too short, but don't you think it adds to one's character?"

A grunt of an answer comes from the boy.

"What are you studying right now?"

"You're not allowed to ask me that," he snaps.

I swallow down a growl and peer around the side of the booth to find them both with their masks off. Theodore, who faces in my direction, holds his black and red reptilian mask in his hand and is scowling at Anna.

"Oh, sorry. I just got excited, I guess. We are going to spend our lives together, so I just thought we could try to tell each other stuff. Like friends?" Anna admits.

"Friends? Why would I want to be friends with you? I'm already stuck with you as a wife for the rest of my life. How much time do you want from me?"

I see the faltering smile fall from Anna's face. Replaced by quivering lips eyes welling with tears threatening to spill over. Something in my gut twists at her expression. I take a step forward but force myself to stop.

"You're just an immature kid. No wonder your parents held you back from coming to these meetings as long as they did. I don't even think you're ready to come to this one today. Just my luck to be paired with you," Theodore sneers. He takes a step closer until he and Anna are nose to nose and bunches his fist into the front of her dress to hold her there. Anna doesn't blink as she looks up at the taller boy. "You have a little over ten years to pull yourself together, Anna. Until then, stay out of my way."

He pushes her back and, to her credit, she only stumbles slightly. Her face transforms into that familiar emotionless mask our followers wear so well, but on her, it looks wrong. Hot anger lances through me at the open display of aggression.

Theodore Henry just put himself on my shit list.

"That's more like it, *wife.* I'm sure you'll need all the years you can get, so don't waste them." Theodore turns his back to her before putting on his mask and heading towards the tent.

Anna stands there unmoving, and I hold my breath as I watch a single tear roll down her face. With my resolve breaking, I rush forward- straight to her. Her eyes swing over to me, and she jumps, causing me to freeze.

"Oh, it's you. You're the boy from earlier. The one on the balcony." Her voice trembles. She reaches up and wipes her cheek as she gives me an unsteady smile.

My blood freezes in my veins. What did she just say? The boy from earlier?

I stand, gawking at her while she stares right back at me. Her green eyes are more dazzling up close. More time than I thought must have passed than I thought because she speaks up again.

"Hello?" Her voice is a little stronger, but still comes out unsure.

I clear my throat. "Um, you can see me?"

Her eyebrows pinch together while her nose scrunches up. "What kind of question is that?"

A laugh escapes me. Well, even if she can't see me, she for sure heard me.

"Are you making fun of me?" she asks, trepidation tingeing her voice.

"No! No, forgive me," I blurt. "I was just- never mind. Sorry for troubling you." I turn to head away when she stops me.

"Wait!" Her hand grabs onto my arm. "I don't mind if you stay."

I turn back to see her eyebrows pinching together as she studies me, and I resist the urge to smile. "Really?" I ask, quirking a brow at her.

She nods. "I could use some... company," she replies reluctantly.

"Well, lucky for you, I have extra company to spare."

A small smile forms on her lips, but that's not good enough for me. The echo of the anger I felt earlier still clings to me, and I need it gone. I want to replace it with something better.

I inch closer until I can smell the hairspray that's layered in her hair, and then I lean even closer with a conspiratorial grin. She eagerly leans forward, and I whisper to her. "How about we keep each other company for a ride or two?"

Anna's smile turns into a full grin, splitting her face, while her eyes glint with mischief.

"On one condition," she says, biting down on her lip.

"Hm, that is?"

"You tell me your name."

Huh. Guess I may have forgotten to share that information with the excitement of everything. "Ciarán," I tell her, holding out my hand.

"Anna," she says as she grabs with her small, rough hand. It surprises me enough to look down and turn it over. There are dozens of scars and half-healed cuts all over leading up her arm.

"Umm, knife lessons." She gives me a sheepish smile, and I laugh.

Right. The curly-haired idiot kid said she is behind in training.

"Come on, Trouble. Are you ready to ride some rides?"

She nods excitedly as I pull her towards the merry-go-round with the hand I planned on never letting go.

the night before

PRESENT DAY

I PERCH ON MY window seat as I stare out into the inky night. Our house is in the middle of nowhere, secluded from the busy world around us. It is nice to be away from the city. While it is where most of our hunting is done, it is too noisy for my taste.

I am taking a break from my plans. So far, everything is set up for Robert. The last of the snags in my plan had finally been worked out. I just need to make sure that he does not have any big schedule changes, and then I'll be good to go.

This is one of my favorite parts of the hunt. Checking everything off my list as things begin to fall into place.

It is also the most important part because the ending is where mistakes can be the most obvious. This is what makes us different from other untrained killers. I can't afford to make any mistakes. Even though I am excited, I can't let that distract me from my process.

My neck prickles as a familiar sensation of being watched settles over me, but as my eyes scan the area, I see no one. A frown tugs my lips down, and my brows furrow together. I know what it feels like to be watched, but there are some days I feel it constantly and no one is ever there. It makes me wonder if maybe I'm just tired or crazy. Maybe just a mixture of both?

My phone pings, and I look down to see my brother's name pop up on the screen. A smile replaces my frown as I text him back.

Happy almost birthday, Anna bug.

Tomorrow is the day. A party is to be held in celebration of not only my twenty-first birthday, but also my official engagement with Teddy.

My gut churns at the finality of that thought. That knowing that it is about to get very real.

It is supposed to be an exciting time, so why do I feel worse? Was this not what I was looking forward to? Cementing my future with someone and having them to share my life with?

I sigh. At least I have Robert to look forward to. I know he won't let me down.

I get up from my favorite seat at the window and stretch before taking a leap, flopping onto my bed face first. A yelp escapes me when my head collides with something solid.

Wincing, I sit up, rubbing my forehead as I look down to find a small black box. I reach for it and flip it over to inspect it. I find no markings or note of any kind near or on the solid smooth box. A pleasant scent drifts from the item. Something smoky that sends a shiver down my spine. A memory of something I can't quite reach flits through my mind, but is lost before I can grasp it.

Should I open it? Technically, my birthday is still a day away, buuuuuuut who would just leave a present here expecting me to wait to open it?

Deciding that's the right way to go, I pop it open, and my eyes widen in surprise as I do. The most beautiful ring I've ever seen stares back up at me. A silver and black marbled band with a giant black oval cut stone sits right in the middle. On either side of the middle gem are three smaller emeralds. I take the ring out and put it in the light, watching as the stones sparkle. The ring feels solid and cool in my hands.

Could Teddy have sent this to me? How would it have gotten here? I know it's not from mother or father. They would never gift me something so nice, no matter the occasion.

Before I am able to question the origin of the box any further, a beep rings in my room, signaling my parents requesting my presence downstairs. I quickly put the ring back in the box and put it on my dresser before heading downstairs. When I get to the bottom of the steps, they are sitting in the living room and I join them, sitting on the opposite couch.

"Anna, we must talk to you about tomorrow," my father says. I don't say anything, waiting for him to continue on. "Your birthday is tomorrow, and you will need to be ready to leave right after. Have you spoken to Theodore?"

"No, sir," I answer.

"Hmm. Well, I've been in contact, and he has sent me the address of your new house. He says everything is ready for you to move right in."

A mixture of excitement and nerves twists in my gut, but my practiced emotionless mask stays perfectly in place as I answer my father. "Okay."

He looks me over once before nodding his approval. "How is your work, Anna?"

"Steady as always. We hired a new girl. Today was her last day of training. I'm all good to go for my vacation these next few weeks."

"Very good. I'm glad you're able to get away. This transition is a significant time for you and Theodore. It's very important that you both spend time away together and learn all you can about each other."

Another twist in my gut almost makes me flinch, but I fight it before nodding a response at my father.

He eyes me a moment longer before continuing on. "And your hunt?"

"Right on schedule. My methods are meticulous as ever, and my work will be complete before the end of the month." Now, this is something I am excited about.

"Your thirtieth, if we have been counting correctly."

"Yes, sir."

"Fine work, daughter. On this schedule, you will continue to make your family proud. I'm sure your betrothed will feel the same." My father praises with an unwavering tone. "Have you eaten yet?"

"Yes, sir."

"Very well. Give your mother a kiss, then head off to bed. Tomorrow will be a big day for you."

I do as I'm told and kiss my mother's cheek before heading back up the stairs for one of the last times in my life. This house may be the only home I've ever known, but I know I won't miss it after I'm gone.

she is all mine

PRESENT DAY

MY EYES BORE INTO the window, willing the girl to show back up, but she won't. She never does what I want, the brat.

The urge to break open the damn thing and drag her ass out of the house is all-consuming. It would be easy, too easy. I can be in and out with her in my arms in less than a second. The scenarios and possibilities rushing through my mind are overwhelming.

I have been away for too fucking long this time. My jaw clenches hard enough that I actually feel a molar break, but even the pain isn't enough to distract me.

Azrael, my father, stepped down from his position a few years ago, placing me in charge of The Society, and I must be present at every meeting. Luckily, they are scheduled together for the most part, but that means I'm away from Anna longer than I want to be.

The lights turn off in the room.

I'm about to make my move when she appears again at her window seat. My heart leaps as her presence soothes something deep within me, allowing my body to relax a little more. I let my tooth stitch itself back up, and with that, the ache disappears.

Anna would be hard to see on a cloudy night for anyone else, but not for me. I can see her bright green eyes staring up at the stars, something she does most nights. I know how much she loves looking at them.

She lifts her head, exposing her neck to me in a silent offering, beckoning me to come and taste her sweet skin. I instantly get hard and have to adjust myself. I can't wait to have her.

Her soft lips move as she names the constellations that are visible tonight. I watch her instead of the stars she admires so much, captivated by the woman I've been obsessed with for eleven years.

She stays there for an hour. A few times she looks directly at me, her eyes narrow as she tries to locate me. I'm sure she can feel my gaze, which never strays away from her, but she won't find me. Not unless I want her to.

After she goes to bed, I wait an extra half hour before I make my move.

With just a thought, I'm in her room less than a second later. Standing at the edge of her bed, I study her features, which are soft with sleep. Her chest rises and falls steadily with her breaths. I am completely surrounded by her scent, which is sweet and floral. It beckons me closer.

Before I know it, I am crawling into her bed and pulling her into my arms, like I have done for years.

At first I was fine with staying outside and watching her, but then the obsession progressed and that wasn't enough. I needed more. I always needed more of this woman who has me in such a chokehold and doesn't even know it.

Tucking her closer to me, I drop my head and trail my nose up her neck. Anna lets out a soft moan, and I growl in response, hugging her tighter. The possessive demon side of me taking over and wanting to own more of her. More than what I have already stolen from her.

I have never crossed any lines with her. No. I need Anna to be awake. I need to see her desire for me with my own eyes first.

She wraps her arms around mine to secure them more tightly around her, and I pause when I catch sight of her hands. My pulse stutters when I see her finger and notice the ring on it.

It's not just any ring. It's *my* ring.

My muscles tense as the darkness creeps in and takes over. The feral demon who wants nothing but to lock away his pretty prey and spread his wicked love to the thing he desires more than anything else. I swallow hard as I fight my instincts, fight for control to not hurt Anna.

Now that she is wearing it, I know that she has chosen me. My black heart swells in my chest, and I make a silent vow, thanking the devil himself for his blessing.

For giving me this temptress and allowing her to accept me. I will treasure her always.

I turn the beautiful woman over in my arms until her soft breath fans my face. My hand moves up to cup her face, and I run my thumb over her soft cheek and down to her plush lips. I push harder against her bottom lip, dragging it down. Her breath stutters at my possessive touch, and I wonder why I torture myself by riling up my devilish side. Maybe I am just a glutton for punishment.

I fight the demon within me, who wants nothing more than to take and possess every part of Anna Wilson. I know she won't wake up. She never does. Instead, her body curls further into mine as she seeks more of me. More of *my* warmth. Chasing *my* touch. Wanting *me*.

Today is her birthday and the day she moves in with Theodore Henry.

At least that's what she thinks.

That asshole doesn't deserve her. Not a single one of her fucking breaths belongs to him.

No. They are all mine. She is all *mine.*

Very, very soon, I am going to steal her away. First, I will punish her for her behavior these last few years.

Once I am satisfied, I will give her everything she has been missing out on and will ever need again. Then, I will make her feel like she can't breathe without me.

i feel safe & happy

BACK THEN

A SHRIEK TEARS OUT of my mouth as the beat-up kiddie rollercoaster flies down the biggest drop on the ride. It can't be more than a ten-foot drop, but I have never experienced a rush like this before. My stomach swoops down before flying back up and steadying as the ride turns sharply.

Ciarán laughs next to me, the sound making me giddy and causing the giant smile plastered on my face to spread impossibly wider. His warm hand lies over mine as I keep a death grip on the rail. I might have actually been frightened a bit of the ride if it wasn't for him keeping me company. There is something about him that is calming to me. Like he is the moon pulling the soft tides of the ocean and, more than anything, I want to be the stars in the sky beside him.

All too soon, the ride comes to a jolting stop as the brakes hiss and squeal as they slow us down. Ciarán does something that causes the bar to pop up, and he jumps out of the cart. He holds out his hand for me, his smoky gray eyes piercing me as he stares expectantly at me. I chew on my bottom lip as I take his hand and let him help me out.

He sticks his tongue out at me, and I erupt in a fit of giggles before he tugs me along towards another ride. As we pass the ticket booth, I catch a glimpse of myself and come to a halt as I see my wild curly hair a mess on my head, and no bow.

"Oh no," I whisper.

"What's wrong, Trouble?" Ciarán says as he stops next to me.

When he first gave me the nickname, it had made me feel kind of fuzzy and warm. But now that ice chilled my veins, it brought no such feelings. A small frown pulls at his lips before I can answer. Temporarily struggling to get myself under control, I am about to start my ritual of naming the constellations when Ciarán's hand moves to my face.

"Anna, talk to me."

I close my eyes and take a shaky breath, breathing in his smoky scent before opening my eyes again. "My bow. It's missing. Father and mother will be upset," I croak.

He nods at me, dropping his hand from my face and instead holds onto my shoulders so I have to face him. "It's okay. It probably fell off on one of the rides. We will find it, don't worry, okay?"

I sniffle and nod at him. Having complete faith and trust that he means what he says. "Okay."

"I can find it faster on my own, so I'm going to leave you here. Don't leave this spot. I'll be right back."

I nod again. He squeezes my shoulders, and I watch his body shimmer before he turns, sprinting away from me.

Huffing out a breath, I shift on my feet for a few seconds, then decide I need to be still. I need to quiet my mind, but so much has happened in the last hour I can't make the thoughts stop.

Even though I am having fun with Ciarán, I'm not supposed to be. It's supposed to be wrong, but it doesn't feel like that. I feel safe and happy with him. Being with him is nothing like being with Teddy. I have only been alone with him for fifteen minutes, but I already know he hates me.

Teddy is going to be my husband, but he was mean to me. He doesn't want me. Doesn't even want to be my friend. He looked at me as if I was gum on his shoe. Was that who I am going to spend my life with? He said he'd tolerate me if I changed. Maybe I'll just have to work harder to do that. That thought alone makes me want to cry. Stupid Teddy. Why couldn't Ciarán just be my husband instead?

Soft footsteps on dirt sound from behind me, and I feel a familiar presence. I turn, ready to find him holding my bow up in victory, but my smile falters as I realize the presence feels different and is over-whelming.

"Expecting someone else?" A deep grumble of a voice asks from the darkness. I tilt my head up and look into Ciarán's eyes. Well, they aren't exactly his, but they are so similar. The only difference is these are cold and laced with danger.

Fear claws at my throat, causing me to swallow hard. Shadow members don't feel fear. I immediately straighten my shoulders and put my well-trained emotionless mask back on my face. "No. I am not," I answer, lifting my chin.

The man stares back down at me, his lip ticking up. "Oh, child. Do you think you can get away with lying to me? I'll give you one more chance to correct your mistake."

Not knowing what else to do, I try to change the subject. "Who are you?" I ask in my best stern voice.

His smile widens before he answers. "Isn't it obvious?"

"If I had thought so, I would not have asked." Technically, not a lie. He could be anyone.

"Hmm. Why don't we have Ciarán explain that to you? Come here, boy."

I recognize his aura, but despite the similarities, Ciarán's is very distinct. Fighting the urge to turn to face him, even though I really want to, I stay put. I wasn't dumb. Even without his answer, it was obvious this is his dad.

Ciarán comes to stand next to his father. His face is expressionless. His gray eyes stay locked on mine, conveying a cryptic message behind them.

"Tell Anna who I am," the man demands.

Ciarán swallows subtly before doing as he is told. "This is my father."

"Do not be obtuse, Ciarán. Tell her who I really am," his father hisses.

An uneasy feeling goes through me before he says anything. A second before he confesses, I realize his eyes are pleading with me.

"This is my father, Azrael Balor, the ruler of the Devil's Shadow Society."

My perfect emotionless mask cracks open as my face morphs into shock and disbelief. "So that would make you…"

"Yes. A demon."

it's time to leave

PRESENT DAY

I TWIRL IN FRONT of the mirror, wearing my dark green birthday dress. The day is finally here, and everything is more than perfect.

This morning I woke up feeling amazing and refreshed. It has been a couple of months since I slept that well. I was sure my nerves would have made me sleep awful, but luckily that wasn't the case.

A sigh of pure contentment falls from my lips. Good days like this, I hope, will be an everyday occurrence once I'm Mrs. Anna Henry. Today, my first day of being officially his is such a high note already. This has to be a good sign. Right?

The buzzer in my room goes off, letting me know it is time to leave. I go to my dresser and slip on my new ring that matches my dress perfectly and head downstairs without a second glance back at the bare room.

"Oh, honey, you look just beautiful," Mrs. Henry says as she pulls me into a hug.

"Thank you." I smile back at her.

"Happy Birthday, Anna," Mr. Henry says as he gives me a firm handshake.

I shake it, giving him my thanks before turning to Theodore Henry, my soon to be husband. Something flashes behind his eyes before he relaxes his features, smirking. He pulls me into a hug, capturing me in his strong arms. His bright blue eyes stare down at me, a brown curl flops onto his forehead. He presses me closer.

"Happy Birthday, betrothed," he whispers into my ear. "I can't wait to have you to myself soon."

A shiver runs down my spine, and a dark laugh comes from him before he pulls away. Who is this version of Teddy, and is this what I get to look forward to? Maybe my doubts about him are wrong after all.

Even as I think that, I'm not so sure.

"There are many guests you need to meet, honey! Why don't I take you around and introduce you?" Mrs. Henry says. My attention goes back to her, and I nod, letting her pull me away, but not before I turn back to Teddy. He gives me a wink before he heads away with his father.

We go through the hotel conference room, which is tastefully decorated. Family and Shadow members greet me and offer their congratulations and best wishes. Out in the public, I am allowed- or better put- required for this celebration to openly show my emotions, which I happily do.

After what feels like an eternity, I feel a big hand on my shoulder and I spin on my heel to find Mason standing before me. He picks me up and swings me around in an over the top show of brotherly love that he would normally never do.

My brother is more naturally reserved, unlike me. I know he does it for my benefit, and nobody is going to shun him for it. I laugh in his arms, but all too soon, he gives me one giant squeeze before he puts me back down on my feet.

"Mase! Oh, I've missed you," I say to him.

"It's been too long, Bug," he agrees.

We pull away, and I see Hazel, my brother's wife, standing close by. She gives me a small nod, and I pull her into my embrace. Startled, she takes a moment to return the hug, but gives me a sweet smile when I pull away. "Hazel, it's so good to see you!"

"It's good to see you too, Anna," she replies gently.

While my brother and I have almost black curly hair, hers is pin straight and light brown. She has big brown eyes and appears as calm as ever. I am dying to know what her kill signature is or even who she hunts, but I think I will probably die before figuring it out. All I know is that I like her, and so does my brother.

"Where's Teddy?" Mason asks.

"Umm, somewhere? There's so many people we have to talk to. I'm sure he's just busy." I force a laugh, ignoring the twinge in my gut. Mason purses his lips slightly before giving a small quick nod, not pushing the subject.

"Anna, honey! There's some people over here I'd like you to meet," Mrs. Henry exclaims. We are in one corner of the giant room, but it sounds like her voice came from somewhere in the middle.

"Ah, speaking of duties, I've gotta get back to it," I sigh.

My brother gives me a teasing grin before I roll my eyes and head back to my future mother-in-law.

Not used to being around so many people, I am feeling overwhelmed. I trace my ring, letting myself be grounded by the feel of the stones in the unique band for a moment.

I'm about to move forward when someone bumps into me. A cold dampness seeps into my dress, and I look down to find a large stain growing. Confused, my eyes trail up to find a tall, beautiful woman with a long blonde, slender ponytail and tight fitted red dress staring down at me.

"Oops. I didn't see you there. You should really watch where you're going," she snarks.

Stunned, it takes me a moment to register what has happened. I open my mouth to say something when a familiar head of curly brown hair cuts straight toward me. I close my mouth and smirk while I wait for Teddy to come and handle the situation.

He looks upset. The corners of his mouth turn down, and his brows furrow together. His blue eyes appear icy and darker than usual. He comes and stands right in front of me.

"What's happened, love?" He asks, pitching his voice low.

Okay, well, the pet name is new. I'm really loving this affectionate side of Teddy today. Before I can say anything, the girl basically throws herself at him.

"She's just awful! She pushed herself into me and caused me to spill wine all over her!" she cries.

Unable to control myself, my face twists up as I try to process what it is I'm seeing and hearing. Why is this woman lying? Who is she? What the fuck does she think she is doing to my future husband?

"Shhh. There, there. Do not cause a scene, Nicole." He soothes, putting his arm around her tenderly before turning his icy gaze back to me. "Is this true, Anna?"

"Wha- no! It is not. What is going on here, Teddy?" I whisper harshly, motioning to this Nicole woman who he was comforting instead of coming to my defense, his future wife.

"None of your damn business, that's what. Now I will deal with you when you get home. Do you understand me?" His tone is colder than usual. The threat is obvious as he addresses me.

Now this is the Teddy I am used to, but after experiencing his tenderness he has shown me he is capable of, the sting of his words cut that much deeper.

My gut sinks. How can he be so cruel to me? How can he blatantly be so disrespectful towards someone he's supposed to spend his life with?

Yet as the anger swirls inside of me, I can sense another emotion. Relief. This is my way out.

I'm about to tell him that my understanding is me calling off our union when a tall, deliciously muscular man stands in front of me, cutting Teddy from my view.

His concern is etched onto his handsome features- his strong jaw flexing while his dark gray eyes pierce me.

My heart stutters for a moment as his smoky scent fills the small space between us. Why is it so familiar? Before I know what I'm doing, I find myself leaning closer to him. Like I can't help but be drawn in.

"Are you okay, Trouble?" His deep voice rumbles.

What did he just call me?

back to hell

PRESENT DAY

ANNA IS BREATHTAKING. BEING so close to her while she is awake is so much better than when she is asleep. I watch her facial expressions change before me as her anger morphs into surprise, then finally a flash of desire settles behind her eyes. Her body leans closer to me, and whether it was intentional or not, it makes the demon in me run wild.

Damn it all. Nothing compares to this woman. I wonder...

"Are you okay, Trouble?" I ask, testing the waters with the nickname I gave her so many years ago.

Her eyes widen in surprise before she narrows them and tilts her head. "What did you call me?"

I chuckle softly, and her mouth pops open. "Well, you look like trouble to me. Does the name bother you?"

She hesitates before she shakes her head. Her hair falls over her shoulders with the movement. Unable to stop myself, I grab at the strands and twirl them around my finger.

"Um, do I know you?" She breathes. Her gaze stays locked on me. When she doesn't shy away from my touch, I take that as encouragement. "You seem... There's something that is familiar about you."

"Hey! Get your fucking hands off my future wife!" Theodore hisses. He moves closer towards us, but I ignore him and continue my conversation with Anna as if nothing is out of the ordinary. This is my first time speaking to her in years, and I plan on enjoying the moment, no matter what.

"Hm, why do you ask?" My voice steadily replies even though the proximity of Anna makes me volatile.

Anna's attention is being drawn behind me to the angry asshole, and jealousy rears its head with anger hot on its tail. How dare she look at another man when I am in front of her? How dare *he* even think he can speak to me that way?

"It's fine, Theodore. He's just helping me," she gives him a clipped response.

I drop the soft curl and ball my hands into fists to restrain myself from snapping the Henry's only son's neck in half. He is ruining my moment with Anna, and if he pushes his luck, he will not live long enough to regret the day he was born.

"It doesn't look like that," Theodore snarks. I turn around to find he has forgotten all about his whore and is trying to get to Anna. He is a few inches shorter than me, but that doesn't seem to deter him- our trained killers know no fear.

I try to stay professional and push my instincts down. Way down. Painting my best charming smile on my face, I look down at him. "Please rest assured, Mr. Henry, the stain your second-rate hussy caused the woman of the night will be taken care of. In fact, the stain is setting, and we are causing a bit of a scene. Please tend to your guests while I tend to Anna."

I all but purr the last sentence and watch as murderous intent flares in his eyes. They shift behind me as if wanting to see *my* girl, but I will not allow that. She will never be his. In fact, he has just lost all rights even to look at her.

Grabbing Anna's hand, I pull her until she is out of view from him. She follows me easily, and I usher her forward so we can head out the door and into the hallway. The party continues on, Theodore opting to save face instead of trying to stop me from taking Anna. Big mistake on his part. Little does he know, he will never see her again, if I have my way.

"Um, hello?" Anna says. "Where are you taking me?"

I turn around and notice the range of emotions on her face. She is so vulnerable and open with me in this moment, and watching her makes my breath catch. While she studies me curiously, a hint of a smile hangs on the corner of her lips. In contrast, sadness seems to permeate the surrounding air.

I'm on the verge of storming back over, second-guessing my decision not to break Theodore's neck, except that she holds my hand firmly in hers and I don't want to let go. I step closer to her. Her breath hitches as she watches me, and I relish in these sensations that are *her*. Changing my focus lets some of my anger dissipate, if only momentarily.

"I'm taking you somewhere safe, so you can get cleaned up," I answer. My voice is gruff as I try my best to rein in my demon.

"Oh okay. And you are?" She stands in front of me with one eyebrow raised as if to challenge me, but it's counterproductive since her hand is still in mine.

Fighting a smile, I reach down to cup her small face. She is so small compared to me. I just want to keep her locked away and all to myself. "Do you not know me?"

"Well, since this is the first time I've met you, and I'd definitely remember someone as hot as you, then I'm going to have to say no. I do not know you."

My lip twitches up, her eyes trailing the movement. She licks her lips, and I swallow the groan that rises in my throat as well as shoving down a hundred sinful things I want to do with that tongue and mouth.

"Oh, you think I'm hot?" I tease.

Her cheeks blush, but she doesn't shy away. "That's what you got from that? Figures."

I chuckle again, loving every moment of this.

"Are you going to answer me or not?" She squeezes my hand, and in response, I give her cheek a little pinch. Her nose bunches, and I swear I can see her fighting the urge to stick her tongue out at me. Oh, thank the devils. They blessed me with a feisty brat.

"Maybe if you're a good girl, I will." I move my hand from her face and see a glint of mischief in her eyes a second before she catches my hand and pulls it back to her face. Captivated, my eyes stay trained on her as she brings my thumb to her lips and gives it a bite.

It was a little harder than was necessary, but still playful. She gives it a small kiss and looks up at me through her lashes. "Did you not know?" she purrs. "I'm not a good girl. I'm one of the bad ones."

Fuck. Me.

Without warning, I scoop her into my arms and send us whirling away where nobody can take her away from me. Back to my home.

Back to Hell.

every. single. sinful. inch.

Present Day

There is something so familiar about the mysterious man who showed up at my party and saved me. His scent and his presence should have been threatening. Danger rolls off him, evident in that predatory gaze and vicious smile.

Yet, I feel safe with him, which is alarming. I know nothing about him, so what is wrong with me to make me feel that way?

I'm supposed to be a trained killer. Playing on people's emotions and desires to get what I want is something I've practiced and perfected with ease. So when I saw my opportunity to do so, why did it backfire on me?

When the handsome stranger protected me from my asshole of a fiancé, who I will declare as my now ex-fiancé, I saw his possessiveness over me. While I want to use it to my advantage, it has stirred something inside of me.

Desire.

When he gave me an opportunity to rile him up further, I didn't know that I would be getting caught up in the feeling, too. That that *need* would grow into a hunger. Nothing like that has ever happened to me before, and I, for once, wasn't in control over what I was feeling or how my body was reacting.

Just who is this perfect stranger? And why does he look at me like he wants to burn the world for me?

He holds me to his chest, his dark gray eyes staring down at me. I'm in a trance, becoming consumed by his gaze alone. I don't even notice we are somewhere completely different.

He's walking with me and only looks away when we reach a door. With the break in eye contact, I blink away before following his gaze and frown when I don't recognize the decorative architecture surrounding us. "Umm. Where is this?"

"Home," he answers in that deep, rich voice that makes my clit pulse.

"Where is *home* exactly?" I prod, but he doesn't answer. I'm instead distracted as I take in the delicate carvings and details of the "home" he claims is his. Although it is more like a mansion than anything else. I have never seen such a beautiful or elaborate home before. I gasp as my eyes bounce from wall to ceiling to floor, as no corner is spared. "This is where you live?"

"Sometimes. Are you hungry?" His change of subject is abrupt, but I let him pivot the conversation.

"Um, yeah. I could eat." I move to get out of his arms, but his grip only tightens on me.

"Where do you think you're going, Trouble?"

Again, another bolt of electricity shoots through me, but I bite the inside of my cheek as I do my best to ignore my arousal. Just what kind of spell does he have over me? I need to put some space between us before I do something embarrassing. "I can walk just fine. Last I checked, my legs still work."

His free hand wraps around my face to grasp my jaw, squeezing it as he brings his face closer to mine. "Is that an attitude you are giving me?" he whispers.

An intensity burns in his gaze, causing a shiver to run down my spine and the flutters low in my belly to transform into a raging storm. He is testing me, pushing me, and I want to push him right back. "Maybe it is. Is that a problem?"

"A problem? No, Anna. It's actually better this way. That way, we can start on what's long overdue."

I swallow, my mouth feeling way too dry. "What's that?" I rasp.

He doesn't answer, instead letting go of my face. With his long legs, he strides down a hallway before turning down another. He opens the door and kicks it shut behind him before heading straight towards the largest bed I have ever seen.

I let out a squeal as he tosses me down, and I bounce onto the soft bed. He watches me as I lean back on my elbows and stare at him.

"What are you doing?"

"You know what I'm doing, Anna."

I shake my head. "But we just met, and I was just engaged to Ted-" before the words escape, the otherworldly handsome man is leaning over me with his large hand covering my mouth. He moved so fast I didn't even have a chance to blink. The force he uses knocks me from my elbows, but he doesn't advance any further than that.

"Don't you dare finish that sentence," he growls. "After you saw him soothe and comfort another woman who attacked you, leaving you to look like a fool. Choosing not to help you. Choosing someone else instead? Do you think that worthless man deserves you? Huh, baby? Do you really dare to say another man's name in front of me? Because I assure you, you will be punished if you push me like that."

Feeling a tangle of emotions inside me, I don't answer.

He's right. I know he is. Teddy has never treated me right, and I always make excuses for him. If he can move on, then so can I. Maybe this man is using him as an excuse to get hate sex out of me, but damn, I will let him.

Right now, the only thing I can think about is how my body responds to his and how there are too many clothes between us. Surely that isn't right for someone whose chosen mate is another? So if that is the case, what reason do I have for holding back now?

"Anna, I'm going to move my hand. You be a good girl and remember what I just said, okay? You already have a punishment lined up for tonight, but don't push your luck. Okay, baby?"

I nod slowly before he lowers his hand from my mouth.

"What's your name?" I ask.

He smirks. "I'll only answer that on one condition."

"What's your condition?"

"You have to promise to scream it all night. Can you do that?"

My breath stalls in my throat, and my face flushes. His smirk grows to a grin before he lowers his body onto mine, and I feel every. Single. Sinful. Inch. Of this man. I let out a small groan, and my breath quickens.

"Trouble, I'm going to need a verbal yes or no before we continue," he warns as he ever so slowly shifts on top of me. He is being serious, but the way he looks at me lets me know he knows what he is doing. Desire's flame turns into a roaring fire as my clit thrums to life. My body is demanding attention, and I am a total sucker.

"Yes. I agree," I gasp.

He chuckles darkly before he drops his face into the crook of my neck, running his nose and lips over the sensitive skin. Goosebumps erupt everywhere our skin touches. He stops at my ear, his lips brushing over me as he finally gives me an answer. "My name is Ciarán, and you better make sure those lungs are working good enough to scream."

good girl

PRESENT DAY

Anna is fucking divine.

I have her.

She's here with me, and soon I'm going to hear her screaming my name from those tempting lips for as many hours as I can get. It's not going to be enough. It won't ever be enough to make up for the years I've lost with her, but it's a start. I'm going to make her feel pleasure until she cries. Until her pleasure turns to pain. Until she begs me to stop.

But will I?

No.

She will take and take and *take* until I want it to stop. *Only* when I say. I want to make sure she will never forget me. Never again. I want- no- *need* to brand myself onto her just like she is branded on my black heart.

Anna bites her bottom lip as I press my body further against hers. I love the feeling of her body responding to me. How I can feel her growing needy for me and my touch. She stays there waiting for me. Ready for me.

Well, almost ready.

The problem is there are too many damn clothes between us.

In one swift movement, I jump up and rip her green dress down the middle. She gasps as she tries to move her hands to cover her exposed skin, but I tsk at her before grabbing her wrists, holding them above her head.

"You don't want to be in any more trouble than you already are, do you?" My eyes stay on hers. I watch her pupils dilate as her chest begins to rise and fall quicker, with her breaths growing harsher. Anna hesitates, watching me keenly, and I fight my urges to be rough with the brat. She isn't ready for that demon side. Not yet.

"Anna, don't make me ask again."

"No," her answer comes out in a gasp.

"Good girl."

I slowly drag my eyes away from her face and suck in a sharp breath as I see her laid out before me. She isn't wearing a bra, so her perfect, fuckable tits are out on display. A strangled groan leaves me as I trail my finger down her body. Anna shivers beneath my touch as I relish the feeling of her smooth, soft skin.

When I get to her lacy pink underwear, I don't hesitate to shred those too, causing her to gasp.

"Hey! Those were my nicest pair." My eyes flit back to her face.

"You are no longer allowed to wear underwear around me, so I don't see the issue."

She scoffs and rolls her eyes. "Okay? And what about when I'm not with you? Do you just expect me to go commando or something?"

I think about telling her she will never be away from me again, but then in less than a second my mind races through the thought of her being around anyone else without underwear and the original thought of her wearing "her nicest pair" for someone else.

Forgetting my previous resolve to cherish her body and slowly devour it, I am instead blinded by a possessive jealousy. I snap my fingers, and her hands and legs are instantly bound to the bed, her body now laid bare, at my mercy and inviting me in. With a snarl, I put my mouth over her already wet pussy and let my tongue punish her for me.

She tugs insistently at her restraints as her body arches off the bed. She screams my name, and it's the best fucking thing I've ever heard. Taking her curses and pleas as encouragement, I quickly send her over the edge in less than thirty seconds.

"Fuck, Ciarán!" True to her promise, she continues to cry and curse as my tongue moves at a demonic speed over her clit. Wanting to see how many times I can destroy her in the first thirty minutes. My guess is at least ten, but I have high expectations for my girl. I am sure we can do better than that.

She jerks as she comes beautifully on my tongue for the third time. Her body is now coated in a sheen of sweat, and where the ropes restrain her, I can see them cutting into her skin. I want more still. I need more of me marking her and owning her.

I decide that since she is being such a good girl screaming my name, I will slow down and let her have a second to catch her breath before we continue on. Picking my head up, I replace my tongue with my fingers so I can slowly stroke and tease her swollen, glistening pussy. I look down at her, with her eyes closed as she pants, trying to catch her breath.

"Look at me, Anna," I growl.

With a whine of protest, she does what she is told and looks right at me. "What kind of devil are you?" She breathes. I almost stop stroking her as I throw my head back and let out a deep laugh. Her lips tick up into a lazy smile, and she lets out a small sigh of contentment.

I lean over her. "Oh, baby. You have no idea," I whisper conspiratorially. She stares up at me, and her brows pinch together. "What's wrong?" I ask.

"Well, it's just that I'm here lying naked on your bed, and you're all, you know, touching me, but you still have your clothes on."

"Oh? Do you think you've earned your chance to see all of me already?" I taunt.

Her flushed cheeks flame brighter as she bites down on her lip. It's cute that she is trying to act shy, like she isn't tied to my bed and I didn't just have my head between her thighs. I bite back another laugh as I decide to comply.

"I'm warning you now, Anna. Once my clothes come off, I'm going to have a harder time holding back from you. Do you understand what I'm saying?" She nods her head in eagerness, and I can't help myself. I lean down and kiss her gently.

It's then I realize in my haze, I completely skipped our first kiss and went straight to kissing her other lips. Better late than never.

Her kisses are perfect. She lets out a small moan, and I deepen the kiss. I lick the seam of her lips and she parts them, allowing me to explore her mouth with my tongue. She lets out a sound of surprise, probably tasting herself on me. I chuckle as I pull away and step off the bed.

"Okay, baby. Time to show you your birthday present."

tell him the truth

I CAN'T TAKE MY eyes off this man. My body is the most alive I've ever felt, and I kill people as a lifestyle choice, and that gives a high like nothing else does.

I've never believed in God. My family may worship demons and devils, but I am pretty sure that he has nothing to offer me that this man won't give me. I will let him be my new religion. I'll only send prayers to him if he is going to worship me like this.

Ever so slowly, he undresses. First, it's his shirt that he pulls off, exposing his perfectly toned chest and abs that pair perfectly with his broad, muscular shoulders. My eyes drink in every exposed inch, trying to memorize everything in case this is some lucid-filled dream.

Next are his pants, and while I can't see much below mid-thigh, thanks to how he has me tied up to the bed, my eyes remain trained on what matters. The large bulge in his underwear that strains against the material.

"Oh, baby, are you sure you're ready for what comes next?" Ciarán asks. His voice is husky and dark, but I can tell he is teasing me. He can probably see the way my arousal drips between my thighs onto the bed, anticipating what is to come, and he won't have missed the way my mouth basically waters for it. For him.

I swallow hard and force myself to look away from his underwear up to his eyes. "Yes. *Please.*"

He half-closes his eyes as he lets out a groan. "Oh, Trouble. You begging? You're going to be my undoing," he rasps. His jaw muscles twitch, and his skin looks like it ripples slightly before he opens his eyes, and I see that possessive fire come back tenfold.

His underwear burns off him. They actually *burn*, leaving nothing except his exposed large cock. I gasp at the show before focusing on the dick that is surely about to destroy me.

A dark chuckle comes from him as he palms the massive thing. If it isn't a foot long, it is damn well fucking close. "What's wrong, baby? Don't tell me you're getting cold feet? Because I'm not letting you get away from me."

I am pretty sure I am about to be fucked by a literal demon. I don't know how he came to be, or what he is doing, being obsessed with little old me. Not knowing if I am ever going to get this chance again, even though his sinful mouth keeps making promises, I decide not to think about anything other than this moment. I am going to have to make sure I remember everything I can before I have to go back. Back to Teddy.

Something about that thought makes my emotions burn the back of my throat. I try to rein it in, but realize I fail miserably as my eyes burn. Before I can do anything, Ciarán's hand is on my jaw as he forces me to look up at him.

"What's wrong? What has you making such a face, when you were so excited moments ago?"

I shake my head, trying to get out of his grip, but he is much stronger than me, and doesn't let go. "Anna," he growls. "You have five seconds to start talking or else I'll start making you scream," he threatens.

I cannot get myself under control. Something cracks inside me, and my emotions spill out. A sob escapes, and less than a second later, my arms and legs are free and Ciarán is cradling me to his chest, soothing me.

Here I am, about to get the best sex of my life, and I ruin it by turning into a crying mess.

"Shhh," he soothes. "It's okay. I've got you, baby."

He picks me up and, leaving the bed, he takes me into another space. Not a few moments later, the sound of rushing water hits my ears. He slowly lowers us into a hot pool of soothing water. Never letting go of me, he alternates between stroking my legs, back, and arms, keeping me tucked close.

After a few minutes, I quiet down and start hiccupping. Ciarán gives me a glass of water from seemingly nowhere that I greedily chug. Once it's empty, he takes the glass from my hands. Before he can say anything, I bury my face in his neck so I can avoid him seeing me.

"I'm sorry." I rasp, my voice raw from crying.

His arms band around me, and I let out a sigh, feeling safe and secure in his arms. His fingers go back to stroking my spine. "Talk to me, Anna," he pleads. After a minute of not saying anything, just enjoying the sensations, he tries again. "Anna, please."

Slowly, I lean back. I wipe my face a bit and look up at him. He doesn't look mad, just worried. Not wanting to see that look, I make a decision that goes against everything I've ever been taught. Something that goes against my very being as a killer raised in the Devil's Shadow Society- I bare my soul and tell the truth to a total stranger.

"It's just that I'm pretty sure you're a demon or devil of some kind, and I'm just a girl who isn't special or anything. Yeah, I've had some sex, but I'm not even that experienced, and since you are and can literally have anyone you want, I know you can't possibly want me the way you said. But for some reason, thinking about leaving you is hard to think about." I take a shallow breath before continuing.

"I was just thinking that I was going to have to remember this as best I can because it isn't going to last and how I will have to go back to my life and... *him,* and that just makes me unbearably sad. There's some sort of connection I have with you. I can't explain. Like maybe a part of me knows you or recognizes you? It just feels right, and I've never felt like this before."

I laugh humorlessly. "That sounds crazy. Confessing to a stranger how I feel about them. How can I feel safe, protected, cared for, desired? We've just met, but I don't want this night to end, so that's just why I started crying and ruined sex and the moment and everything."

My cheeks burn from the admission, and after the first sentence I can't meet Ciarán's eyes. The shame of sounding like a love-obsessed teenager is too much to bear, so I just stare at a spot on his chest as I- for the first time in my life- relay out loud what I am feeling to another person.

"Is that all?" he asks. His voice is deeper than normal. A small threat of something laced in his tone.

I bite down on my lips as I hesitantly nod, bracing myself for the rejection that I'm sure is about to come. For the criticism I'm sure to receive, because I am crying over someone I just met. For him to send me away and maybe even steal my memories of this beautiful night, if that is something he has the ability to do.

All these scenarios are playing in my head, so imagine my surprise when he lifts me up and roughly slams me back down on his large dick. It doesn't go in all the way, maybe only a few inches, but I straighten up as a scream of pure pleasure rips from me.

mine.mine.mine.mine

RELIEF WASHES OVER ME, knowing that my precious Anna isn't crying because of me. She is upset at the thought of this being only a moment in her life. Something fleeting and not meant to last more than a night. The thought of her leaving me is crushing her, and that fact alone makes my own black heart swell.

Silly girl.

Maybe the issue lies with me? I thought I was telling her and showing her what she means to me. How I don't want to let her go, but I was holding back after all. It was time to let him out. My demon side that wants to keep Anna Wilson all to ourselves more than we need to breathe. More than we want to live. We want to possess and own every part of her forever. If she doesn't get that, then we are just going to have to show her.

The time of holding back ends now. I open the door to my heart and let him out. My skin ripples as my black skin coats my body. I feel my two black horns tipped with silver escape from my skin. My fangs elongate, mirroring my horns, ending in silver.

The change happens in less than a second, and in even less time than that, we have Anna held up right where we want her before slamming her down on our cock. The overbearing need to have her taking over us. Her tiny body arches back as she lets out a scream, the sound music to our ears. With a groan of pure pleasure, we pick her back up and bring her back down over and over, getting deeper and deeper.

With my demon out, it's only seconds before we are totally one being. One being with our sole focus on the beautiful girl in my arms, who my dick was currently inside of.

"Look at me, Anna," I growl.

Her eyes snap to mine. They widen for a moment before I impale her again and her eyes begin to roll to the back of her head. I wait until they refocus back on me.

"You are it for me. Do you got it, baby? I'm not leaving you, and you aren't leaving me. Not. Ever." I continue to fuck her as I talk to her. She tries her best to listen, but I can tell her attention is focused on something else.

Maybe I should have planned that better? Oh well.

"This pretty pussy? It's *mine*. That sweet mouth of yours? Mine. Your heart, your soul, your every breath and word that passes over those perfect lips? Mine. Mine. Mine. *Mine*." I make my point by thrusting after every claim to her. I can feel her close to coming, her walls clenching hard around me. Shit, she feels so fucking good. I won't be that far behind her. "That orgasm you're about to have, that's all mine too, baby. Don't you worry about not having me because I'm all yours. I'm more yours than you'll ever know. Do you understand me?"

"Yes!" she screams, not missing a beat. "Fuck! Yes! Ciarán, I want to be yours."

"That's a good fucking girl. I want you to come for me now. Give me what's mine, Anna."

Just like that, she falls apart, my name a prayer on her lips.

Not a second later, I feel the familiar tingling of magic shooting through me. I come with a roar, following my girl over the edge, but continue to move my hips at a punishing pace as I make her body take everything I have to give. I smile like an arrogant asshole when she comes again without me even trying. My girl is just so receptive and in tune with my body.

"You're so fucking perfect, Anna. You're never going to get rid of me. There's no escaping me now." I whisper against her lips as I pull her into a kiss.

"I can't imagine a world where I would want such a thing," she says as she pulls me closer to her, deepening the kiss. I growl, pulling her into a bone-crushing hug. She giggles sweetly. A smile pulls at my lips as warmth spreads through my chest.

So this is what feeling whole is like. This is what it's like having the woman I've been dreaming about and watched for years. It's so intoxicating, and I already know it isn't going to be enough. Still inside of her, I give her a few teasing thrusts, which she laughs and swats at me for.

"Down, boy. As much as I'd love to do that again, I need time for a full recovery."

"You know there's more we can do that doesn't involve that exact anatomy, right?" I taunt, going back for another kiss. She kisses me back, moaning softly as my hands explore her body.

I pull away and see a tiredness around her eyes. The part of me that cares about her wellbeing more than my desire for her comes back in charge. My black skin recedes as I fight my demon and suppress more of him, so I can think clearly. The fangs and horns will fade eventually, but I don't focus on that as I get some shampoo and body wash to clean her.

"So you can control it?" Anna asks, her hands trailing over my skin.

I grunt an answer as I focus on taking care of her and less on my wound-up body, but damn, is she making it difficult.

"How does it work? Does it hurt?"

I catch her hands as they trail down my stomach. "Trouble, wasn't it you that was too tired to keep going? Hm? So why are you testing a demon's resolve? I promise it won't end well for you."

The brat laughs at the warning I give her, but she does behave and keeps her hands to herself while I finish bathing her and then myself.

"When are you going to tell me everything about you?" She asks when I pull her out of the water and wrap her in a towel.

"Tomorrow."

"Ciarán," she warns as she stands defiantly with her hands on her hips. I watch as the water drips down her freshly fucked body before she slowly dries off. I clench my fists at my side.

"What did I just warn you about?" I growl.

She smirks as she whips off the towel and, in one swift, calculated move that only a trained killer can pull off, she wraps the towel around my outstretched hand and pops me with the other end of the towel.

"That's it!"

Anna's eyes widen as she squeals, taking off running towards the bedroom. I catch her before she can make it and jump into bed with her. She wiggles underneath me as her laughter surrounds us. I lay flat on her, pressing her further into the bed, the same position we were in only an hour earlier.

"Now, now. What punishment best fits the crime?" I ask as I flash her a smile with my fangs still on full display.

"Do your worst." She smiles up at me.

"Oh, baby. Say less."

dream come true

WARMTH EMBRACES ME, AND my body aches all over. With my eyes still closed, I roll onto my back and immediately regret it. I let out a hiss as my sore ass meets the bed. My eyes pop open as I try to orient myself.

Bad idea. Abort!

A deep chuckle rumbles from next to me as I roll back onto my stomach. I grab the nearest pillow and chuck it at Ciarán, whose gorgeous naked body is lying next to mine. He easily evades the weaponized pillow and instead grabs me, pulling me closer so he can plant a kiss on my lips.

My groan of protest easily melts into a moan of pleasure as his skilled lips soon have me breathless. After a few minutes, I realize my body is not ready for this repeat of events. I plant a hand on his firm chest and push him back, but it's like pushing against a wall.

"There a problem, Trouble?" he asks against my lips, not allowing me to have the break I am seeking.

"More like a concern. My body has already been destroyed. Just what are you planning to get from this?" I mumble.

Ciarán hums as if he were contemplating that, but his tempting lips still devour mine. "There were no complaints last night."

I open my eyes and find him staring down at me. His gray eyes sparkling with a mixture of amusement and desire. This devil is going to be the death of me. I push back again, weaker this time, as my head starts spinning. It's like he is trying to punish me with kisses. "Trust... me. I'm paying for... that... now." I manage to get out, narrowing my eyes at him.

Instead of letting up, he advances, and I let out a small whimper as he leans over me, turning me to the side-onto one of my very sore cheeks. Another dark chuckle rumbles from his chest, and a spark of annoyance flares through me.

Before I chicken out, my lips are quickly replaced by my teeth as I bite down hard on his lips and part of his tongue. I twist my head sharply, feeling a tear of flesh. Soon after, blood pours into my mouth, and I'm forced to swallow a mouthful of his smoky blood before I unclench my jaw, letting go of him.

His chuckle turns into a full on laugh. My eyes stay locked on his, but instead of seeing anger at the action, I see nothing but a flame of pure lust burning in his eyes.

He pulls away slowly. My eyes follow his bloody tongue and lips as he licks the black blood away. Transfixed, I watch before letting out a small gasp of surprise, seeing the skin completely healed as his tongue swipes across the area. My eyebrows shoot up.

"Something wrong, Trouble?" His laughter dies down, but his eyes still hold nothing but desire.

Swallowing the thick lump in my throat, I shake my head but pause when I feel a lightness to the movement. I frown, confused, and lift my arm up, realizing the earlier aches in my shoulders are gone. I inspect my wrists and see no evidence of the bruising from being tied up. My jaw falls open, and my eyes fly back to Ciarán's face for an answer.

"What just happened?" I ask.

His face twists in confusion as his eyes trail over me. In one swift motion, he lifts me back up by my ass to straddle him. On instinct I wince, expecting pain, but am pleasantly surprised when there is none.

"Hmm. Maybe I've turned into a genie and granted my own wish for another pleasurable day?"

"Do genies exist?"

Ciarán's lips quirk up into a smile, but he doesn't say no.

Interesting.

One moment I'm straddling him in bed, the next I am in his arms as he walks us to the bathroom. Pouting, I wrap my arms around his neck and give him my best puppy dog eyes.

"None of that, Trouble. You'll get more of me later tonight. Right now, we have business to attend to." His eyes stay locked with mine as he walks us through the large stone bathroom and back into the warm pool we used last night.

"*We* have business to attend to?"

"That's right."

"And what business is that?"

"It's a surprise," Ciarán says with a secretive smile. I roll my eyes, but feel no anxiety or worry in his presence.

He finishes bathing me, slapping my hands away when I attempt to help or wash him, so I just sit and enjoy the feeling of his hands on me. Once we finish, he flashes us back to the bedroom.

"Well, I know you don't get that body of yours through walking," I tease.

Ciarán smirks. "Walking is for humans, Anna. Does that bother you?"

I frown. "No. It doesn't bother me, but how can I appreciate the goods?"

"The goods?" A small crease forms between his brows.

I give him a taunting laugh as I take a few steps away and add an extra swagger to my hips, letting them sway from side to side. I look over my shoulder to see his eyes glued to my ass and laugh again.

Ciarán's hand comes up to scratch his chin. "You may be on to something with this walking thing," he mumbles with a smile on his lips. "Okay, now we really are running late, Anna. Be a good girl and get dressed."

"Or what?" Quickly, I spin on my heel, still completely nude, and place my hands on my hips. I am stalling, and I know it. I love being in this bubble, and I'm not ready to leave to face the reality of the outside world.

I know what he promised, but I also am not stupid and know there are things beyond us that still affect us when we leave. I'm sure there is only so much that even a powerful devil can control.

My emotional side has taken over since I have not needed to rein in any of my emotions while being with Ciarán. This is like a double dream come true, as he doesn't judge me for saying what I want or showing how I feel.

In a flash, he is in front of me, and throwing me over his large shoulder. I squeal and barely have a chance to throw out my hands to avoid faceplanting into Ciarán's perfect ass.

"Wait!"

"Oh no, Anna Wilson. The time for waiting is over. I gave you a chance to be a good girl, but you didn't take it," he taunts, his voice deepening in a sexy threat. His large, warm hand rubs over my ass. My core clenches at the sound of his voice as a small thrum shoots straight to my clit at the anticipation of what is to come.

A second later, I hear the smack before I feel the sting from the full force of his hand coming down on both cheeks. I let out a cry as my core clenches harder on nothing. Immediately his hand is back, rubbing away the sting of the pain. We get back to the bed, and he sets me down. Grabbing my chin, he tilts it up until I meet his eyes.

"That was a warning, brat. You thought you were sore this morning when you woke up? Just wait until tonight," he promises. I see his skin ripple, flashing me a hint of the demon that is ready to come out and play.

I lick my lips and smirk.

"Can't wait."

this fine dinner

It takes every single ounce of self control to not say "fuck it" to today's plans and teach my little troublemaker a lesson.

This will be good for us. I know she can't hide her true feelings from me. Now that I know her worry is losing me, I understand her hesitation about leaving. She is afraid to risk what is between us. Not that she has anything to worry about. We need to leave so I can show her.

When I promised to protect her, I meant it. I am going to do everything in my power to keep her safe. Absolutely nothing will keep me from her.

Anna walks into the closet to finish getting dressed with the clothes I bought her. I knew what she'd want and love based on what I'd seen her window shop for and wear recently. She now has an entire closet of clothes here at *our* house.

"The clothes!" she exclaims.

"Is there a problem?"

"No, that's the thing. I love them." She comes back out and looks at me. A wide smile spreads across her face, showing off two dimples on her heart-shaped face. "How did you know what I liked?"

I smirk as I give her a half shrug.

"Ciarán, really!"

I laugh. "Do you really wanna know?"

"Yes." She walks closer.

"Okay, well. I've just been following you for a while. I've seen what you like and looked at, and every time your eyes lingered on something just a beat longer than normal, I would get it for you."

Her jaw drops open. "How long have you been doing that?"

Closing the gap between us, I stop to study her for a moment. "Me getting you things? Only recently. Now watching you? Forever."

Her throat bobs as she swallows, and a small blush spreads over her cheeks. "You're serious about me, aren't you?" she whispers.

"Baby, I've never been more serious about anything else in my life." If I had a soul, I'd bare it to her and show her how serious I am. Unfortunately, I have only my words, but I mean every one.

Her eyes glisten slightly before she takes a deep breath and blows it out. "Well then, I guess I better get serious about getting dressed."

Anna turns and I spank her perfect ass as she walks away. She lets out a yelp, and I chuckle as she hurries off to change.

She ends up wearing a chunky knit green oversized sweater with black jeans and a pair of designer boots. While she does her makeup and tames her wild sex hair, I also change. I stick with my usual- dark jeans and a black button-down shirt with leather shoes.

Once Anna is ready, I appreciate the way she almost drools as she takes in my appearance. "You like what you see, baby?" I ask her with a smirk.

She wrinkles her nose slightly before coming up and, with her nimble fingers, pops open the top two buttons of my shirt in less than a second.

"Now I do," she replies with a giggle before biting down on that sexy as fuck bottom lip of hers.

Before she can get away, I grab her and pull her back to me. Her green eyes twinkle with mischief, but when I look closer, I can see her anxiousness simmering just below. I reach out and tuck a loose strand of dark hair behind her ear. My finger trails down her cheek, to her chin, then down her neck, and I watch as her body shivers beneath my touch.

I swallow before using my powers to transport us right into my father's foyer. Anna doesn't even notice the change in scenery with her gaze locked on mine. Just as it should be. I always want to be at the center of her attention, just like she has been mine ever since the day I met her.

Knowing I can only stall for so long, I wrap the same finger around the loose strand of hair before giving a playful tug to it. It earns me a smile and playful swat on the chest from my girl, but it also loses me her attention.

She finally notices we are no longer in the comfort of our home, and her body automatically tenses up. I see the well-trained killer come out as she quickly takes in her surroundings and drops the emotionless mask in place. She steps away from me, and I have to fight my urge to pull her right back because I know better than to interfere.

I am sure she found the gift in her closet with the array of her favorite weapons- blades. There were all different assortments, the best of the best, from different worlds and composed of various metals, all for her. She most likely has a couple tucked into her outfit somewhere. Even though they are useless against my father and me, that won't stop her from using them on instinct, and I know how painful she can make the cut.

After another moment of inspection, Anna turns back to me, letting me see that spark of hers for a moment. Her look asks a silent question.

"My father's house," I answer. My eyes remain trained on her face to gauge her reaction to the information, but I see no reaction.

"Isn't it too soon for such a meeting, Ciarán?" she asks with a slight tease in her voice.

I smirk and give her a half shrug. "You're going to do it eventually. Why not now?" I see the slightest of twitches on her lip, but she says nothing else.

"Tell me something about you," she says.

"Hmm. What do you want to know, Trouble?"

"What's your last name?"

Huh. Should've seen that coming. I hesitate a moment before answering her. "You know I'm a demon, right?"

She nods her head yes.

"Okay. You should understand there are different types of demons and families from your teachings. I'm one kind you're more familiar with. My full name is Ciarán Balor."

Her face falters as she stares at me, wide-eyed and openmouthed. She stays like that as she brings her hands to her face. I can only imagine the range of emotions with realizing she just got fucked by the devil she worships.

"Anna, baby?"

She blinks at me for a few moments before dropping her hand and nodding. "Yes, Ciarán?"

"Do you need a moment?"

"No. I'm good."

I smirk. "That's my girl. Come on. Let's go eat. I'm sure he's waiting for us."

Cautiously, I reach for her hand, and she lets me hold it. As we walk down the hall towards the dining area, Anna's hand squeezes mine. All too quickly, we get to the doorway, and she immediately drops my hand. I step forward and walk to my normal seat next to my father's.

I pull the seat out next to me, indicating to Anna where she will sit. She stands behind the chair and waits, and I smile internally at her teachings. She would never sit down before an unknown person walks into the room.

No, my girl is on guard. Now that she knows who was waiting for us to arrive. I'm sure she wants to make a good impression. I stand and wait next to her, while I appreciate her skills and abilities.

We don't wait long. After another minute or so, footsteps quietly approach as someone moves steadily towards us. I suppress a growl as my father's full power walks in like the dreaded being he is- the presence will be overwhelming for Anna. He must have sensed her before he got into the room. I am sure his eyes are tearing into her, daring her to move, but she doesn't. Not a single muscle twitches. Her breath remains steady.

I wish I could have warned her about what was to come next, but I know the traditions. If I want what he has stolen from me, we are going to have to play his games.

Azrael gets to his chair, but still Anna doesn't even look his way, staring straight ahead.

"My, my, son. What a delightful meal you've brought for us this fine dinner."

don't touch him

Back Then

Slowly, I move towards my father, clutching Anna's bow in my hands. I had been so caught up in my time with her, I didn't realize how late it was. Sweat rolls down my back from my neck as I keep my gaze blank.

I hear Anna's pulse increase, but for the most part, she is keeping herself in check. That gives me some relief. I have no idea what my father will do with her when she isn't even supposed to be able to see us in the first place. Yet here she is, doing just that.

What does that mean for her?

My gaze drops to the little girl with the pretty big eyes. For the most part, her face is blank, but her eyes flare with defiance. The urge to grab her and run away to keep her safe burns a pit in my stomach, but I don't do that. I know better than to run. We are just going to have to wait and see what happens next.

"Tell Anna who I am," my father demands.

I swallow my unease that still simmers on the surface. "This is my father."

"Do not be obtuse, Ciarán. Tell her who I really am," he hisses.

My eyes hold Anna's gaze, not sure how she will react to this, but hoping for the best. I need to see what she will do. What she will say.

"This is my father, Azrael Balor, the ruler of the Devil's Shadow Society."

I watch as her face contorts into disbelief. Her little mouth pops open as her eyes widen. "So that would make you…"

"Yes. A demon." I answer her unfinished question.

She takes a moment to collect herself. I see her thinking it over before she gives a small nod, accepting the truth. "Okay."

I arch a brow at her, waiting for more, but only receive a small amused smile.

"Okay?" I finally echo back questioningly.

Anna gives a firm nod, keeping her eyes on me. It is then I realize she has been ignoring my father, and I'm not sure if that is a good or bad thing just yet. These are uncharted waters for me, as this is the first human I've ever interacted with beyond the swift punishments I've dealt out.

"That doesn't bother me. I like being with you. You see me," she boldly admits as a small blush dusts her cheeks.

The smile she gives me makes my stomach flip. Warmth spreads through me at the admission, and whatever feelings I have for her lock into place. I knew then that I needed forever with this girl.

Immediately, the atmosphere shifts as my father's overwhelming presence dominates the space, despite us being in an empty carnival. I shift forward towards her, knowing it is a mistake but unable to stop myself from doing so. Anna is still a human and needs protection from my father, the demon her family and so many other killers worshipped.

I spin around, keeping her behind me as I face him. An amused but cold smile spreads across his face. Anna's hand grips my shirt, and I straighten my back. Azrael's dark gray eyes glint with a cruel amusement, but that is the only shift in his otherwise neutral face.

"Oh, son," he admonishes. "You know better than to make such foolish decisions, and yet here you are not expressing that knowledge."

I don't rise to the bait. Giving no sign that I am even listening to him. I am not scared of him. I know I can handle whatever painful thing he throws my way and that my body will heal on its own. It might be slow, but it will speed up as I get older. I flex my hands that only an hour ago were bleeding from digging my fingernails into my palms, now fresh scabs lay over the skin.

What I do feel is fear for Anna. I'm not strong enough to win a fight against my father if he goes after her, and my gut churns at the thought of him even touching one hair on her head.

He takes a step forward, and I take one too, moving closer to him. A warning growl leaves my throat as my skin ripples. His eyebrows shoot up in surprise.

"What do you think you are doing?" he asks in a deadly tone.

"Don't come any closer," I warn through gritted teeth.

In less than a second, he has me by the collar up against the booth.

"You dare threaten me, Ciarán?" His voice is dark and threatening, but his eyes still hold a glint of something I can't read.

Before I can answer him, a movement behind him catches my eye. A second later, my father's body jerks as something glints out of his neck. Azrael's eyes widen in surprise, and his grip on me loosens enough for me to escape.

I don't hesitate. Anna is still standing behind him, with a feral look on her face and another knife in her hand. I immediately grab her, but she doesn't budge.

"Don't touch him," she says in a low voice, her eyes on him. She might not be a fully trained killer, but even at her young age she could pass for one with the death glare she gives Azrael Balor, the demon she worships.

Being less gentle, and only caring about her safety, I tug on her with my full strength and finally have the ability to pull her away. I'm about to run, but should have known better. The seconds I lost being gentle with her cost us, and I am immediately met with resistance. A glance back at Anna shows me that my father is the cause.

He pulls her out of my grip, and a small grunt of pain escapes her at the force. His huge arm bands around her, securing her in his arms. The full force of his powers is exerted on us, the power so thick as he taps into Hell's miasma- a known toxin for humans.

"No!" I yell out, but it was too late. I can see it now. Anna will never be mine.

a new direction

PRESENT DAY

MY MIND IS GOING a thousand miles per minute, but I keep it together. Never before have I been so proud of my skills as a well-trained killer before.

Not even that time I hunted down and killed Gilbert James- my seventeenth kill- the man who had gotten away with not only stealing millions from a children's home for foster girls, but abusing those innocent girls as well. The fucker thought he had gotten away with it, but he just didn't know he had painted a beautiful, bloody red target on his back for me. All those poor girls who went hungry and cold in the hundreds of homes across the east coast had suffered because he was a greedy bastard, but I made sure he paid them back tenfold with his life before I anonymously gave that money back.

No, not even when compared to this moment, because I know I am in the presence of not one, but two devils. I let my guard down around Ciarán, but I know that with his father, I need to show my best, and my best are my killer skills. The skills that come second nature to me. These skills that honored him and the line of devils who came before him.

He is going to test me. He is testing me now as I stand here, feeling the full weight of his gaze on me. His presence is more than suffocating- it is pure poison.

Still, I keep up the appearance of calm and collected as I wait. When he finally does speak, I allow myself to slowly turn my head to fully look at him.

"Do you have a name, girl?" The older Balor demon asks.

Names hold power. They hold your identity and, therefore, your life. To give it up so willingly to someone you didn't know is a risk. I don't have a choice with Ciarán, as he knew my name before I spoke to him. I am sure the other devil in the room knows my name, but I know better than to just hand it over to him.

"Do *you*?" I ask, letting a small amount of snark into my question.

Maybe I should be more cautious? I am speaking to an actual demon, one I haven't fucked. Yet, I stand my ground. I was taught to think of myself as being the best and most important being in a room at any time, and I am going to keep practicing that belief until my dying breath.

His gray eyes darken, roaming over me as if weighing my very soul with his eyes alone, but his face remains impassive.

"How rude of me," he purrs. In an instant, he is next to me. I am still standing behind my seat, but find myself now sandwiched between two powerful beings. Without flinching, I turn to face him and his outstretched hand. "It's been so long since we've had company at dinner. Azrael Balor, Ciarán's father. But I'm sure you know that."

Azrael towers over me. He looks muscular like Ciarán but slimmer. Both of them have gray eyes and dark hair. The only difference is his father has a more angular definition of features. There is no denying they are related, but do devils even age? I see no sign Azrael is any older than Ciarán. Actually, now that he is closer, they can totally pass for brothers.

I study him a little longer before flashing him a smile. "Anna Wilson." I take his hand and firmly shake it. He keeps hold of it for longer than necessary while his familiar but distinct smoky scent wraps around me. I resist the urge to wrinkle my nose and force down a sneeze. "Your home is lovely."

He raises a brow at me, then drops my hand before walking back to his seat. Azrael sits down, and we follow suit.

For the first time, I risk a glance at Ciarán and find him sneaking a glance at me. His eyes show a depth of emotion, and I have to look away before my mask cracks. Being so open for so long unchecked is making it harder for me to control. It is like these feelings are tethered to Ciarán. Anytime I am with him, they are ready to pour out of me too easily.

What does that mean for us?

"So, Ciarán. Is she ready now? Is that why you brought her?" Azrael asks. He snaps his fingers, and the side doors open. Less than a minute later, there is food being placed in front of me. It looks delicious, and I am hungry. The last meal I ate was last night at my birthday dinner.

Wow, was that last night? So much has happened in a day. My whole life has definitely taken a turn. I am so focused on my food and that train of thought that I almost miss what is being said.

"She's more than ready," Ciarán answers. His warm hand goes to my thigh under the table and gives it a gentle squeeze.

Aaaand I am done for. I smile at him, letting my hand fall onto his.

"Is that so?" Azrael pauses a moment to look at me, and I realize my mistake. I am an open book for him to read. It is like everything I have ever been taught is gone, with nothing to protect me. "So you handled her husband?" His brow ticks up.

My hand tightens over Ciarán's.

Azrael laughs. "No, of course you didn't. Oh, son. You know better than that."

"He's on the damn 'to-do' list," Ciarán grumbles.

"So why wasn't he at the top of the list?"

"He's broken the tradition. He was going to-"

"It's not your job to interfere. Only to observe and deal with punishments. You know what happens when you abuse that power."

I have no idea what is going on, but from the sound of it, Ciarán did something wrong. The food sits in front of me, almost untouched, as I watch the demons interact. I know there isn't much I can do, but I let my free hand drop and finger the large knife that is hidden in my knee-high boots.

Despite the extra hostility, it almost mirrored how my own family interacts, and I wonder if serial killers are more demon than human. That thought doesn't bother me as much as I thought it would. Maybe I am too desensitized.

"This was the right call," Ciarán says. "I'm not sending her back to him." His hand tightens over my knee, squeezing almost too hard.

"And if it's not? Are you ready for the consequences? Because this time I promise you I won't be as lenient," Azrael threatens.

If that isn't a big enough clue that something is wrong, then I don't know what is. My eyes shoot over to Ciarán, and his jaw flexes as he clenches his teeth. A swell of panic bubbles inside me, but I force myself to swallow it down. He promised we would be together, and he is going to keep that promise one way or another.

stolen away

Back Then

My breath stalls in my lungs as my father holds Anna. She doesn't look scared. No, this wildcat is fierce and ready to fight tooth and nail. I see her swift fingers move, and a second later, something glints in her hand as she maneuvers another knife into her hand. I lunge forward to come to her aid, but am only able to watch as she stabs my father.

Azrael winces slightly before he twists the knife out of her grip, and it drops to the ground. I am only an arm's length away, but in the next heartbeat, his hand wraps around her throat. I freeze in horror as I watch his hand flex, squeezing.

"Stop!" I yell. "Don't hurt her!" I sound weak. Killers don't beg. *Demons* don't beg. So what does it mean that I am doing both?

Anna's eyes widen. Whether it is at my outburst or because of the large hand that encircles her throat, I can't be sure.

"Don't come any closer," my father warns.

I lift my hands up in surrender to show that I am going to comply, but then things take a different turn. His eyebrows shoot up, and he materializes with her right in front of me.

My forehead scrunches in confusion. "What did you just do?"

Humans shouldn't be able to teleport with demons. Anna should have stayed in the spot while my father came to me. My father blinks at me for a moment before staring down at the girl in his arms. Other than the cute scowl on her face, she is unharmed.

He lets go of her throat. "I'm going to put you down. If you run or scream, I will hurt Ciarán, not you. Do you understand?" he tells her.

"Yes," Anna answers, keeping her gaze on me.

As soon as he lets go of her, she jumps into my arms, and I catch her. She buries her face in my neck and takes a deep breath, sighing as her body relaxes into me. I hold her close but stay alert.

"What's going on, Father?" I ask.

Anna releases me and moves to stand by my side. I reach for her hand and hold it firmly while I wait for an answer. He studies us but doesn't answer my question.

"Anna, when did you first see us?" he asks her.

"In the meeting," she answers steadily.

"Where were we sitting?"

"Above us, in the booth. I could see Ciarán better because he sat near the front."

Azrael's brows furrow together as he makes a noise of acceptance. "Ciarán, let me see your hand." I waver before doing as he asks, lifting my hand up to him. He takes it and drags a finger over my scabs. "These. When did you cut yourself?"

"I was squeezing my hands tight. I think maybe it's just been a long time since I've seen a pairing ritual. The power was overwhelming for me, and my nails cut into my palms. I didn't notice I was bleeding until after the announcement of the..." I pause before gritting out the rest of the answer. "The announcement of the pairing."

"Of course, the crystal," Azrael mutters before turning back to Anna. "What happened when you talked with your betrothed?"

She squeezes my hand, and I squeeze back encouragingly. It only happened an hour or so ago, so the emotions of his rejection are still raw.

"He was upset with me. I think-" she pauses and takes a little breath. "I think he hates me."

Azrael nods, accepting the answer. "And how do you feel being with Ciarán?"

She turns to me. I give her an encouraging smile. She blushes slightly before turning back to him. "I like him. I wish he were my mate instead of Teddy. It feels right being with him."

My heart skips at her confession. I turn more of my body to look at her and see her blush brighten under my gaze.

"Son?" His voice makes me look back at him. A slight smile plays at the corner of his lips. The curiosity to know what he is thinking burns through me. "I'm assuming you also feel strongly about the girl?"

"I do. I want to see her smile and keep her safe. Mostly I want- well, now it's more like a need- to keep her." With my admission, I pull Anna closer to me until my arms encircle her shoulders.

My father's eyes bounce between the two of us before a smile breaks out over his face.

"Well then, I believe a congratulations are in order. It sounds like you have yourself a mate, Ciarán."

My jaw drops to the floor. "Anna is my mate?"

Could this be a test? Is Azrael just being cruel? For us, cruelty comes as easily as breathing, but he's never shown that side of himself to me, his son. My knowledge of the matter says demons and humans have the possibility of being paired, but it is extremely rare.

"But Teddy?" Anna asks. "I was matched with him. It was announced."

Those words cut deeper than I thought two sentences could. I internally wince. Anna shoots me a look, with a small frown on her face, but I swear not a single muscle twitches on my face.

Could she have sensed my distress?

I think for a moment and realize demon bonds are stronger than human ones forged with magic. There are different abilities and possibilities that come with it that affect the pair. It's not impossible for us to feel each other's strong emotions.

"The leader is wrong. He doesn't know Ciarán, or I were there. He only saw Theodore and made an assumption. It was a false announcement. That would explain why the crystal exploded. It wasn't strong enough to handle the power flowing through it. Tell me, Ciarán, would you say her blood affected you?"

I think back to how the power surged through my veins, threatening to come out in an overwhelming wave when she was walking in front of me with the mating crystal bathed in her blood. It definitely wasn't a coincidence. "It did. Very strongly."

"Well, it's settled then. You two are mated."

Anna turns to face me with an earth-shattering grin. Her excitement buzzes through the air, and I can't help but smile back at the sweet girl in front of me. She throws her arms around my neck, and I hug her back with a laugh.

"I'm so glad it's you," she whispers in my ear. "I was so worried before, but I know you'll take care of me. This is like a dream."

"Although…" Azrael begins. My arms tense around Anna. "Nobody can know about this. Ciarán, you know better than that."

"No," I whisper in disbelief. He's right. I should have known better. My eyes trail back to his face in a plea. He looks sorry, but not sorry enough.

"We are demons, son. The entire world cannot know we exist."

Anna pulls away from me. "What do you mean? Ciarán? What does that mean?" Her face twists up in confusion as she looks up at me. Before I can answer, my father grabs her and puts his hand on her head.

"Sorry, sweetie. He wouldn't have had the heart to do this. You're going to have to stay betrothed to Theodore-"

"No!" I yell, cutting him off. I try lunging at him, but with a snap of his fingers, Hell chains shoot up and bind my arms, pulling me down until I'm on my knees. "Father, please!"

"I'm sorry, son. It's for the best. After tonight, she will have no memory of you or of meeting you."

Disbelief and pain crack open my heart. The thought of Anna not knowing me. Of having to live without her is too unbearable.

"NO!" I struggle against the bindings, but it's useless. Anna cries as she stares at me. Her green eyes mirror my worries, but it's her pain and sadness that consume me. "Don't take her away from me! You can't!"

I can only watch on in horror. Anna's lips move, but I can't hear what she says over my screams. A flash of black leaves his hand, and her eyes flutter closed as her memories of me are stolen away.

i'm in hell

PRESENT DAY

"I AM A MAN of my word. If I say he will be handled then he will be. My job is to protect her. You can't seriously think I'd do anything different. She is of age, and you know what that means for them," Ciarán growls. His skin flickers with black as his demonic side fights to burst through to the surface.

Azrael flicks a glance at his son, and I notice a slight downturn of his lips. He returns his gaze to me before speaking again. "Anna, do you understand what I am talking about?"

I shake my head no. I can make an educated guess, but how sure am I of that answer? Less than I'm willing to admit. The risk of failure is not worth a mistake in this situation.

He nods his head as if expecting that answer. "Ciarán, we can get back to this another time. For now, we can enjoy dinner. Your… guest is hungry." Azrael picks up his utensils and begins eating.

Ciarán turns back to me and blows out a sigh. "Sorry, Trouble. Please. Eat." He motions to my food, and I cut into the piece of meat and take a bite. Whatever it is, is delicious, and I am surprised that it's still hot. I continue eating, trying not to think too hard about this conversation now or how it makes my gut knot up.

I'll ask Ciarán later.

The rest of the meal is uneventful. Azrael leads us to his study after we are done, where he and Ciarán speak in a language I don't understand. They pour drinks and offer me one, but I decline.

Azrael sits in a worn, oversize chair that could pass as a throne the way he sits in it. Ciarán opts for the couch and motions for me to join him, which I do. When I start yawning, he sets his drink down and pulls me into his lap. I attempt a protest, but he ignores my words and keeps me there.

Whether it is from the safety I feel, the happy, full belly or the lack of sleep the night before, I soon find my eyelids are too heavy for me to keep open.

I WAKE UP NAKED with a muscular arm pinning me to an equally muscular and naked body. Ciarán's familiar smoky scent surrounds me, so I don't bother opening my eyes. Sighing in contentment, I wiggle closer, enjoying the morning atmosphere.

"Good morning, baby." If I thought his normal voice was hot, his rough, sleep-laced voice was pure sex. A shiver races down my back that sends a zing to my clit. Holding on to my control by the barest of threads, I bite back a small whimper.

His nose sweeps down my neck as he breathes me in and lets out a small chuckle as a breathy moan I can't contain escapes me. "If I remember correctly, I owe you a punishment for that bratty behavior last night."

"Oh, do you?" I taunt.

"Mmm. Don't worry, I'll make sure you want more of these punishments, baby."

With a burst of skill, I twist out from under his arm and throw my legs around his waist, so I'm straddling him. His brows raise in surprise, but there is a glint of humor in his eyes. "Actually, I have things to do," I say.

His warm hands move up and down my thighs as he stares up at me. I bite the inside of my cheek to hold back my smile. The invitation is too tempting. I need the painful distraction.

"So, what were you and your father talking about last night? You know about me and Teddy?" I try changing the sex-filled atmosphere to something less tempting, but what I get is not what I was hoping for.

The room instantly darkens, and a chill curls around me. I let out a small gasp of surprise at the sudden change. Ciarán says nothing, but his grip on my thighs tightens and his soothing movements from earlier stall. His not very well hidden, suppressed anger becomes a living thing in the room.

"Umm, Ciarán?" My voice comes out in a hesitant whisper.

"Anna, what did I tell you about mentioning another man's name in front of me?" he enunciates each word, making the question sound like a potent threat.

I am not supposed to feel fear. The emotion was trained and beaten out of me at a young age. So when the unfamiliar prickling sensation dances down my spine, my lungs have trouble pumping air. Shallow breaths fight their way past my lips as I get snared by a predator's obsidian gaze.

"Anna…"

I swallow. "I have a right to know. It's about me." Hoping my body portrays some semblance of a backbone by default, even if my eyes probably reveal the truth. I continue to stare at the devil beneath me.

Ciarán's hands move up and down my thighs again, but slower and more deliberately. Focusing on his hands allows me to get a proper breath in.

"Unfortunately, this is something I cannot share with you," he eventually admits.

"How is that fair? It sounds like I could still end up with *him*. I don't want that. Let me help." Feeling bolder,

I wiggle down his body until my skin touches the velvet smooth solidness of his cock. His hands immediately grab my waist, preventing me from moving any further, and I smirk.

"This isn't your trial to pass, Trouble. It's my job to handle him. You know it's against tradition for you to touch him." His features soften slightly, and the room lightens up.

"What if he comes looking for me? He knows you took me. To him, I'm still *his*." My lips curl in disgust as I voice the thought.

Ciarán's lip twitches up. "Oh, I wouldn't be so sure about that, baby. There's only one way he's coming here."

"What do you mean?"

"I mean, this is a place a human can't be." His brows raise up, and it takes me a moment to process what he's saying.

"Ciarán, you aren't saying what I think you are. Surely…"

His smile grows. "What do you think I'm saying?"

I gape at him. "I'm in Hell right now?!"

"Where else does a devil live?" He laughs.

Snatching the closest pillow, I hit him with it, and his booming laugh gets louder. He pulls me down towards him as he easily rips the pillow away from me and tosses it away.

"But how am I here?"

He grabs my hand and pulls it up between us. He twists the ring on my finger that I put on days ago and haven't taken off yet. "This ring. This stone is part of a family heirloom. It's tied to me and my blood. It allows you to stay here with me as long as you want."

"*You* gave me this?"

"Well, it was your birthday. How rude would it have been of me to not give you a gift?"

I am speechless. I have dozens of questions lined up, but I don't get to ask them before he continues.

"Plus, any time you want to remember who you belong to, you just drop a little of your blood, say my name and you will be where I am."

I slap his chest. Ciarán flips us over, and I squeal. He gives me a smile that lets me know I have been lured into a predator's trap. His lips hover just a breath away. "In fact, I think it's best we start that lesson now."

I guess my hunting plans are going to wait.

life worth living

CIARÁN'S HAND TANGLES IN my hair as he pulls my head back, exposing my neck to him. The most delicious bite of pain, mixed with pleasure, dances across my scalp as my body thrums with anticipation.

He leans over me, dragging his lips from my jaw down my neck. A soft moan escapes me, and Ciarán presses his body further into mine in response.

My body comes to life as he trails his hot mouth down my collarbone until he finds my breast. His tongue flicks against my nipple, and I arch my back into the movement, chasing more.

I let my hands move towards him as I explore the heat of his body, the strength of his muscles, and the perfectness that is him. I can't get enough.

This is it.

This is what I have been missing, and I finally have it. I have the full attention and love of someone and, damn, if I do not feel more alive than I ever thought I could. I cannot go back to just plain living.

I am not sure if it is just because he is a supernatural being or if it is just Ciarán that can make things feel so amazing. Either way, I am turning into a selfish bitch, and I know I need more.

Ciarán's teeth graze against my nipple before he bites down, giving it a playful tug. I hiss at the sensation, but bring him closer to me, loving the sting of pain. He lets go of my hair and moves his hand to my other nipple to give it attention. It isn't long before my hips move against him.

"Oh, baby. You ready for more?" he purrs.

"Yes, Ciarán. I need more. Please," I gasp.

The devil has me begging. *Begging*. Something I never thought I'd do in my life. But for him, I'd beg for more and never be ashamed of doing it. I know I am safe with him and he would not abuse my trust.

His large hand moves down to my pussy. As soon as I feel his fingers brush against me, my hips buck, demanding more. He sits up before wrapping his other hand around my throat, holding me down.

"Nuh uh, baby. I'm going to make you feel real good, but you need to be a good girl and be patient. I'll tie you down if I need to," he warns.

I lick my lips slowly and watch in satisfaction as his eyes snap towards the movement. I let my hands trail up and down my body before my hands go back to my breasts and give them a gentle squeeze.

A groan leaves him as Ciarán watches me, his gaze thick with desire. I smirk up at him and let my fingers move towards my nipples as I play with myself.

That lasts all of two seconds before he lets out a snarl and shoves two of his fingers inside of me. They slip inside easily, and I let out a cry at the sudden intrusion.

"You wanna play games, Trouble? Let's play games." The ferocity in his gaze stalls my movements, and he takes advantage of my pause.

His fingers come all the way out of me before slamming back in. I moan, letting my head fall back as I get lost in the feeling of fullness.

"That's right, beautiful girl. Take me. Let my fingers fuck this sweet pussy of yours and feel you come over them. I want you to come so hard, I might actually be concerned about my fingers breaking off. Then, I want you to do it over and over again. Let me hear you scream."

Ciarán plays me like a fucking skilled pianist as his fingers move in and out of me. His thumb moves up to my clit as he swirls it expertly, making my muscles bunch as my impending orgasm crests.

Breathing hard, I let my eyes flutter closed before Ciarán squeezes my throat further.

"Eyes on me, Anna. I need to see you fall apart. Don't let me miss my favorite part."

With a groan of effort, I give in to his demand and stare up into his gray eyes.

"What a good fucking girl. Now, do you want to come for me?" he asks.

His fingers slow down as his thumb stalls. He puts pressure on my clit instead, and a whimper escapes my throat.

"What's that, baby? I need to hear you say it for me." He smirks down at me. If he weren't fucking me so good, I'd clock him in the jaw.

"Yes, please. Ciarán. Let me come." I put extra emphasis in my plea and am rewarded when his eyes widen a moment before his demon bursts through his skin.

"Your wish is my command, baby," he growls, his voice slightly deeper.

He picks up the pace on my pussy and clit and not a second later, I'm hurtling into bliss. I come with a scream as he continues thrusting into me, extending my orgasm until it bleeds into another.

My body trembles with effort as my body tries to curl in on itself, but his firm hands on me keep me in place while I pant and writhe through the waves of pleasure.

He finally pulls his fingers free of me before he sticks them in his mouth and sucks them clean.

"Fucking divine," he groans. "I need more, Anna."

Without warning, he flips me over so that I'm on all fours. His thick cock is lined up at my entrance. I gasp at the sudden change, but I don't have long to think about it before he thrusts all the way in. My head falls forward as I arch into the movement. I moan as the feeling of pure ecstasy envelopes me.

He leans over my back as he starts off with slow, deliberate thrusts. His mouth leaves a mixture of kisses and bites all down my neck and back. The sudden change from painful lust to sweet devotion to my body made me burn from the outside in. I pant as my body tightens up.

"Ciarán…" I moan.

"I got you, baby. Don't you worry," he rumbles.

His hand tangles in my hair as he pulls my head back, while his other hand keeps a bruising grip on my hip. In the next heartbeat, he is thoroughly pounding into me. He holds me in place, and all I can do is take it.

It's not long before another orgasm tears through me, and I cry out as he continues at his punishing pace.

"Ciarán! Fuck!" A string of curses tumble incoherently out of my lips as my third orgasm crashes into a fourth.

My body is completely spent, and I am covered in sweat. My muscles tremble with the effort of keeping myself up, and he still doesn't let up. There is a moment where his hips stutter and he lets out a groan, but he just holds tighter before continuing on.

"I can't… Too much…" I pant out.

Ciarán chuckles as he finally lets go of my hair. My head slumps forward before my arms give out. I fall face first onto the bed.

His laughter turns dark. "You think I'm going to let you off that easily? Do you know how long I've waited to have this body?" His hand trails over my skin, leaving goosebumps in its wake. "You're going to give me two more orgasms, Anna, and then I'll let you take a break."

I suck in a breath as I turn to get out of his grip, but I am weak.

He pulls out of me and flips me onto my back. "You just lay back," he purrs. "Let me taste more of that devilish pussy of yours."

My body aches in protest, but the thought of his skillful mouth on me is tempting. "Ciarán, I don't kno-"

He cuts me off with his hand covering my mouth. My eyes widen, and I move to take his hand away but find my hands restrained to the bed. I suck in a breath through my nose before narrowing my eyes at him and cursing him out behind his hand.

Ciarán laughs again before going down on me and running the pad of his tongue all the way up and down my swollen pussy. My eyes roll to the back of my head as I sink further into the bed.

My body is so sensitive, it doesn't take long for his tongue to get the two orgasms he wanted out of me. On my final one, I bite down on his hand hard enough to draw blood. I swallow down the smoky flavored liquid dripping onto my tongue.

He groans, sitting up and wrapping his bloody hand around his cock. Using it as a lube. I watch with hungry fascination as he strokes himself, moving closer to me.

"Open that pretty mouth up for me, baby. You did so good for me. Let me reward you." He stares down at me through his hooded eyes, and I can't help but eagerly open up and stick my tongue out.

"So fucking beautiful. Letting me destroy you over and over again and still ready for me. Fuck, you're perfect."

With that, he comes with a growl and shoves his bloody dick inside my mouth. I greedily suck him down and lick him clean while his fingers massage my head.

A genuine smile curves up his lips, and my breath stalls in my lungs. Something deep within me comes alive, and I feel a moment of total happiness. I smile up at him, and he scoops me up off the bed.

"Come on, Trouble. Let's get you taken care of."

I lay my head on his shoulder as I close my eyes, letting myself enjoy what could be my new life. I barely notice most of my aches have already disappeared.

person of the night

My footsteps are silent as I follow Robert around his work. It is dusk, and nightfall isn't far behind. The days are now much shorter and the nights longer. As a person of the night, this is my favorite time of the year. Now that it's darker, I have more shadows to hide in.

The area is almost completely empty now since the other workers have all gone home for the night. Robert does not have anyone waiting for him. Nobody to go home to. It is the second Wednesday night of the month, which means tonight he will go to the bar off Ninth Street. He is an infrequent regular to them, but I know his schedule better than he does, and I know happy hour is calling his name.

He checks the on-site restrooms and break rooms before locking them up. The security cameras keep him in their sight as he finishes the routine, but they aren't the only ones. He scratches the back of his neck and looks around the area, but he won't find me. Still, I cling to the darker shadows in the spot I hide.

Once he is ready to go, he packs his bag and begins his walk to the bar. The new development is on the edge of town, with the wilderness tucked right up to it. The bar known as Joey's is only a half-mile walk away, while his apartment is further into downtown, but still within walking distance.

I stay far enough behind as he continues on.

Soon, he makes it to the well-loved bar and joins the crowd inside. I give it a few minutes before I go around the corner into the alleyway behind the bar. They never lock the door back here, thanks to this small town's false sense of security. I slip inside and find myself in the familiar sticky hallway in front of the bathrooms. I make my way towards the safety of the busy bar and tuck into one corner.

Tonight, Joey's has a decent crowd. I am pleased to go in unnoticed, but know that won't last long. Once I'm settled, I pull down my hood and unzip my jacket. I'll stand out more being shady. Even though I risk someone coming up and talking to me, I still need to blend in.

Sure enough, a girl alone in the bar seems to attract a couple of suitors. The first couple are creepy, and I shoo them away, but then a normal-looking guy comes up and I decide to use him as a shield.

With one eye watching Robert who sits at the bar chatting away with the bartender drinking his whiskey, I let the guy in front of me, Abe?- honestly I didn't even catch his name- go off about his beer tastes and the car that he works on. I ask some questions and laugh when I'm supposed to. It's easy to dodge his questions about me and focus the conversation on him.

It doesn't take long for Robert to find a pretty girl to chat up, and my attention zeroes in on the inter-action. She laughs along for a few minutes before he says something and she tenses up. She looks immediately uncomfortable, but he either doesn't notice or doesn't care as he continues on. He gets closer to her as she obviously leans away from him.

Now is the time for me to make my move.

"Excuse me, Abe. I'm going to the bathroom." I slide out of the booth, taking my belongings with me.

"Uh, it's Mike?" He calls after me, but I didn't care enough to respond.

I make my way towards the bar and get the girl's attention, who is still trying to get away from Robert. Pulling my jacket back on with the hood over my head, my eyes stay trained on her. Despite seeing me as a cloaked figure, she still leans towards me when I get into her space and away from him.

That she feels safer with a serial killer than a man who can't take a hint says something. She doesn't know that's what I am, and she may not be my target, but the point still stands.

"Take my hand and I'll get you away from him. Just tell him I'm your sick sister," I whisper in her ear. She pulls away enough for me to meet her eye. Understanding mixed with relief passes through her, and she relays the excuse to Robert, who whines.

"Oh, come on! I'm sure she's fine. She can get home without you, can't you, girl?"

The girl stands up, and I pull her arm over my shoulder, before exaggerating a hunch, making it look like I was clutching my stomach.

"No, I think it's best we go home. Come on, Claire," she says before she wraps herself further around me, leading me outside. Robert mutters a string of curses before a glass slams down on the bar. The girl jumps slightly, but I hold her tight.

We stay close until she leads me a block or two away. She steals a glance over her shoulder before pulling away.

"I think the coast is clear," she says.

I glance back too before agreeing and standing up straight. "You okay?"

"Yeah." She pulls her arm back from me and takes a small step back. "Thanks for saving me. That guy started saying some weird stuff, and I was creeped out. I tried backing away, but then he just kept pushing, you know?"

"He's not a good person. You should be more careful," I say.

"I will thanks."

"This your car?" I ask, pointing to a small black car next to us.

"Umm, yeah, actually," she mutters, blushing a little. She heads over to the driver's side but pauses before attempting to get in. "What's your name?"

"Anna," I answer and am slightly surprised that I told her the truth.

She smiles. "My name is Meredith. Thanks again for saving me." With that, she gets into her car and drives away.

Meredith, huh?

I guess that's one less potential victim for Robert F. Giles. Really, I am just doing it for myself. I am so close to making my move. I can't risk any outside factors messing it up.

At least, that is the half lie, I tell myself.

Warmth spreads through my chest when I remember the look that she gave me, and I enjoy the feeling for a moment.

I stay outside and wait for the bastard to come out, which is only twenty minutes later. Robert glowers as he stomps home, muttering to himself. I follow him all the way back, staying a safe distance away.

I wait until I see the lights in his apartment turn on. He gets ready for bed and then, not long after, I see his lights go out. Feeling confident the trash will stay put, I decide I should go home, too.

My fingers trace the black stone a moment before I pull out my small knife in my waistband. I make a superficial cut on my finger before placing it on the ring and think of home like Ciarán had taught me to do. Soon I am whisked away and brought right where I want to be.

Home.

Feeling very good about life, I decide I'll bake myself a cake tonight.

i'll even beg

24 YEARS OLD

THE MEETING DRAGS ON, and I have to force myself to stay put for the entire damn thing. The last two days with Anna, I couldn't afford to miss, and yet I had. She is just so addicting. I wouldn't have been able to leave even if I had wanted to.

I would happily give up my title and responsibilities just so I could spend every second with her, and I wouldn't have a single regret doing that. She is worth the sacrifice, and demons don't make sacrifices.

Unfortunately for me, that is a dream I can't afford right now. The only other candidate is a distant cousin, and spending the years it would take to train that tyrant will take even more time away from her than I'd be willing to give.

Anna's meeting is in a few days. I have to make sure she is going to make it. The only thing now is to figure out whether Theodore Henry is also going to make that meeting. Surely he'd want to take her back from me, but that just wasn't an option for him.

I technically haven't caught him doing anything wrong yet, but I have been avoiding him for years. Especially this last year. I knew if I'd watched him, my control would have been tested beyond my capabilities, and Theodore would have been dead long ago. While it was obvious he didn't stay faithful to Anna, he could have passed it off as nothing with no concrete proof.

Talking with my father about Anna gave me some hope. Only following through with the traditions set in place will let me keep her for myself. If I stray from them, then I risk losing her forever. I'd rather die a thousand deaths than let her go.

Damn, I forgot to ask him about her healing. I'll have to remember that the next time I see him.

A heavy sigh escapes me, and I pinch the bridge of my nose. Nobody can see me here, so I am free to be more of myself without worry. I am distracted, and I shouldn't be.

"As you all know, this is the second month that Peter has been missing." The leader's announcement catches my attention, pulling me from my thoughts. "After his family raided his belongings, it appears more like foul play is a factor in his disappearance. We know that killing one another is strictly forbidden, and if one of you is the culprit, be prepared for the ultimate punishment."

Not another one. Fuck, I don't even know how I have gone so long without realizing someone else had been killed.

That wasn't entirely true. For the last couple of months, I was distracted knowing that Anna's birthday was coming up. I am going to have to send the hounds out to find the body, but I already know it was useless.

They would find nothing on the killer, like all the ones before.

"I have reached out to the surrounding companies and have found that another has gone missing as well. Both different backgrounds and genders, but they have two things in common. One was their age. Both of the missing persons had just turned twenty-one. The other was that they were not paired yet."

Murmurs break out across the crowd.

This I already knew. It is part of the reason I wanted Anna with me as soon as I could get her.

"This is all pretty new, and there's not much, but still be vigilant," the speaker says. The obedient crowd hushes to listen to what he says. "You are smart, capable people. We are here for one reason, and that is to serve our demon lord, Balor. I'm sure wherever they are, they aren't going to waste their time with worshippers who can't even stick with the basics like staying alive. Don't embarrass us."

A smart man. This is why he was chosen to lead his people.

Although the one who should be embarrassed is me. Well, if I could feel embarrassment. All I feel now is anger at the asshole who is trying to undermine me and taking lives that are not theirs to take. These killers' deaths are mine, and whenever I finally get my hands on them, they will have hell to pay.

The meeting ends in a prayer. The swell of power burns through me, making me feel refreshed as I absorb it all. I am going to need every ounce for this hunt and, more importantly, my girl.

I GET BACK HOME as soon as the meeting is over. I need a distraction from reality. The Hellhounds are already out looking for the body of the missing man, so what better way to kill time than by hearing my name echo off the walls by the sweetest of voices?

Anna is in the kitchen mixing something at the counter when I get home. She has her back turned to me, but I notice her muscles bunch up slightly. She knows I'm here.

Slowly, I stalk forward until I reach her and place my arms on either side of the counter, trapping her within my embrace. She doesn't even flinch and makes no acknowledgement of me.

I dip my head until my lips find the crook of her neck and slowly kiss my way down. When I get to her shoulder, I pull down her sleeve so I can continue. Her body betrays her as a shiver goes down her spine, but still she does not acknowledge me.

The demon inside begs and claws to come out and have a taste. Just because she's acting like a total brat, I let him.

My skin ripples, turning solid black as my fangs and horns emerge. My body grows bigger until I am in my fully shifted form. I breathe a sigh of relief at the natural feeling. We merge into one being, and I gladly let his desire for Anna take over.

I may have loved and coveted her, but he obsessed and ached for her in such a devastating way. Our desire for her grows and multiplies into its own demon.

My kisses turn into bites as my fangs pierce her soft skin. I mark her with my teeth and feel her jump slightly, but she continues with her meaningless task. Still. Ignoring. Me.

No. I can't have that.

I need her attention. Crave it. Fuck, I'll even beg for it, if that's what it takes. I immediately push away from the counter and grab the hem of her pants, easily ripping them off. My knees hit the ground as I spin her so that I can make room for myself. In less than a second, my mouth is on that devilish cunt of hers.

Anna gasps as I let my tongue punish her.

"Oh, Ciarán," she moans.

My eyes trail up until I meet those beautiful green eyes. My mouth almost stutters as I see a devious smirk on her swollen lips. Before I can continue on, she jumps away from me.

"Trouble?"

"How about we play a game?" she offers.

"What kind of game?"

"Let's see how good of a hunter you are. If you can catch me without your powers in ten minutes, I'll let you fuck my face. But I get a head start."

"Baby, I don't know if I can restrain myself for too long." I'm still on the floor, looking up at her naked body with her pussy glistening with her desire.

Anna shrugs. "If you can give me two minutes, you'll be rewarded." Her hand moves down her body, teasing me still.

"One hundred eighteen, one hundred seventeen, one hundred sixteen…"

She laughs as she spins around and starts running away.

Anna has no idea what monster she just let loose.

run, baby

My pulse races from the thrill as I take off at a run from the kitchen. Taking off my shirt and bra, I throw them in the opposite direction from where I'm headed, hoping to throw Ciarán off my trail. I can still hear him counting down.

Earlier, I explored a bit of the small mansion, so I know where I want to hide. No point in wasting time or energy being quiet, especially since I am not sure how good his senses are.

I turn down a large hall. There are dozens of art pieces scattered all over the walls, making it seem like something important should be here. Yet, the door is hidden. My hand runs over the wall until I find the concealed latch. It clicks, echoing in the hall, and I wince.

"Oh Anna! Come out, come out, baby," Ciarán taunts.

Shit. I am out of time.

"I promise to take it easy on you the first time if you're good for me," he says.

I smile. Who said I wanted that? I head straight into the dark hall. The door latches shut with a click behind me.

For being Hell, it's surprisingly chilly, making my naked flesh break out in goosebumps. About a quarter of the way down, I hear a noise behind me, and flames bring the wall sconces to life, illuminating the long corridor.

I keep going, my way now more visible. At the end is a door to a massive office. Right as I reach my hand out to grab the handle, the door swings open and a very naked and smug-looking Ciarán stands in front of me.

"Found you," he purrs.

I scream in surprise before turning and running back the way I came.

"You can run, baby, but there's nowhere you can hide where I won't find you." He laughs as his steady footsteps follow behind. His pace speeds up, closing the distance between us.

My spine prickles at his proximity. The exit is just up ahead, but I won't make it.

I slam into the door at speed with Ciarán's body crashing into me in the same second. My chest rising and falling with my quick breaths- a mixture of adrenaline, exertion, and lust. His dick is hard against my ass as he traps me against the door.

He growls, wrapping his arms around me. "Well, look at what I just caught." His breath is hot against my ear, and I arch into him, pressing my ass further back. "I believe I was promised a service for my prize, and I intend on cashing in."

"If you caught me in ten minutes *without* using your powers," I reply.

"Trouble, are you accusing a devil of being a lying cheat? If so, I am a little hurt."

My laugh comes out breathy. "Well, do you want your prize or not?"

"You don't have to ask me twice."

Ciarán spins me around in his arms and lifts me up. His lips crashing into mine as he deepens the kiss, and I moan. I wrap my legs and arms around him. He walks until my thighs bump into something.

"Lie back, Anna," he murmurs.

Unwrapping myself from him, I lean back on my elbows, licking my lips in anticipation as my eyes stay locked with his. I welcome the cool feeling of the table. My body hot with need.

Ciarán slowly walks around the table. The tension between us is electrifying. My clit throbs as I lie all the way back, waiting for him.

He pulls me towards him until my head hangs off the edge. His big hand slides up and down his cock while the other grips my jaw. "Tongue out, baby."

I obey and am rewarded with choking on him as he shoves-almost- all the way in. His thick head hits the back of my throat. I breathe through my nose as I relax my jaw and try to control my gag reflex. From this angle it slides in easily, but, fuck, he is big.

My hands slide up and down his body. One of his hands wraps around my hair, pulling it tight at the base of my skull before it cups the back of my neck.

Ciarán pulls out, and I take a gulp of air. His eyes are almost black, glinting with a dark promise of pain and pleasure.

"Now then. Let me reward you with fucking this pretty mouth of yours. I'll remind you who it is you belong to and how, no matter what, you'll never get away from me."

My tongue swirls around his hard length, stroking him as he speaks to me. Tasting and teasing him as he claims me and my body.

He narrows his eyes, a smirk on his lips, and a shiver goes down my spine. "I'm going to show you what happens to brats who get caught. Don't think I've forgotten about you ignoring me earlier." I smile and hum around him in response, and with that dark promise, he shoves back in.

I am glad to not have a sensitive reflex as he maneuvers my head, taking complete control of me. His hips are all but slamming into my face as he moves me in time with him, and I take what he gives me.

My breaths are ragged and shallow as he gets himself close. My nails dig into his abs where I lay my hands for stability as I moan around his dick.

"Fuck yes, baby. Mark me. I need more of you."

I dig my nails in further, and another muffled moan escapes me when the dark lines turn wet with his black blood. The tension in my body comes to a crescendo as it aches for relief.

As if he knows, his free hand comes to my nipple as he flicks it, and I cry out at the attention.

Ciarán throws his head back with a growl. Then, in the next second, the full weight of him lies across me and his mouth is on my pussy. Bolts of electricity shoot through me as his tongue slides up and down my slick folds before giving my clit a punishing lashing.

It's not long before I'm coming, and Ciarán thrusts deeper as his balls tighten, his own orgasm releasing down my throat.

I swallow him and lick him clean, tasting some of the blood running down and mixing with his cum.

One minute I'm on the table, the next I'm up against the wall as Ciarán wraps my legs around his head. I scream at the sudden movement. Especially with me now sitting on his shoulders, six feet in the air.

"Ciarán!"

He laughs against my core, and I gasp at the feeling of his hot breath.

"Don't worry, baby. I won't let you fall. I've got you. You're just so delicious. I needed more." His hands that are holding me up tighten on my legs.

He steps closer to the wall, and his tongue picks up speed, making me focus only on him. My head falls back, thudding against the wall, my hips bucking as I ride his face and he grunts encouragements.

It's not long before my body tightens up as another orgasm hits me. I come with a string of curses falling from my mouth. Ciarán keeps going, his tongue feeling like it picks up even more speed.

A bead of sweat trails down my chest as I pant against the wall. I try slapping his hands away, but he just chuckles. "Ciarán, *please*."

He pulls back just enough for me to hear him, his lips still brushing against my sensitive pussy. "Please what, baby? Please keep giving your needy body more orgasms? You know how I love hearing you scream."

He shifts me in his hands and inserts two fingers inside me.

"Ciarán," I groan.

"Okay, Trouble. Only because you ask so sweetly. You give me one more, and I'll let you have a break."

He adds another finger, and I gasp out an agreement. After more teasing- prolonging the blissful torture more than is necessary- and his name being cursed and screamed over and over, I come one last time before he lowers me to cradle me in his arms.

"Mmm, baby, you taste like the sweetest sin," Ciarán says as he grins down at me.

My body is sticky with sweat, blood and us. I sigh into his embrace. "Oh yeah? Well, you taste like a devil."

He smirks. "And what does a devil taste like?"

I grab him, pulling him closer so I can run my tongue over his skin. "Delicious," I answer.

A growl leaves his throat before he turns and walks us out of the hall. "I guess you didn't learn your lesson about teasing? Let's start that refresher course again."

I laugh. "How can you want me so much?"

"Anna, you're all I've ever wanted and all I'll ever want for the rest of my life. If you still don't believe me, I'm going to show you after I clean you up."

Warmth blossoms in my chest as I stare up into his gray eyes. My fingers trailing over his jaw.

"I believe you, Ciarán," I whisper.

And at that moment, I can feel that truth.

a rare treat

My new favorite sound is hearing Anna scream my name. If I could make it into a playlist to hear on repeat, I'd be a lot happier when I have to leave her.

Today I don't have to do that. Luckily, we can spend the day together as I show her what her new home is like. She gets dressed in a frenzy as she babbles on in her excitement.

"I can't believe I actually get to see Hell! Is this okay to wear? Do I need to wear specific shoes? What are you wearing? Do I need bigger knives?"

I smile at her. Loving how I can interact and be with her like this. She is perfect, not even remotely scared of what is out there. From the stories humans pass on to each other about what could be here, I would have accepted having to help her with those worries, but no. Anna Wilson is wondering what she should wear to impress the demons in Hell.

"You look great, baby." I come up behind her and wrap my arms around her waist, and meet her eyes in the full-length mirror in her closet. "What you're wearing is perfect. Besides, I don't expect us to see anyone." She wears black jeans with black knee-high boots and a dark green top.

"You're sure?"

"Positive. I mean, this is what I'm wearing. We look similar enough." I motion down to my outfit, which consists of jeans, a red shirt, and leather shoes.

"Okay. Then I guess I'm ready!"

"Perfect. Let's go."

Still holding her, I transport us to the nearest park so we can take a stroll through it. It isn't like normal parks that humans find in their world, but it's similar enough. It is still an open area with places to sit and lounge about.

There are lights made from witch bones, their magic powering them and giving off a blue hue. Large dead trees, scatter around the area that are thousands of years old. This park is near a rocky area, so the far side of the park has large, sharp rocks along the edge.

Instead of grass, it is a soft type of scales, called Grun, that you'd find on a long-extinct type of fish. Even with how large the area is, the amount of scales wouldn't have even covered a quarter of the damned creature. Rainbows glint across the park wherever the false sun hits the Grun. As far as parks go, this one is very mild.

Anna inhales sharply. She takes in everything with her head moving from side to side as she scans the area. She looks back up at me. "Can I touch anything?"

I frown. I hadn't thought about that and wasn't so sure if she could. Just then, a familiar presence appears, and my arms tighten around her.

"My, my. A human in Hell? That's a rare treat," the loud, rich voice says.

"Watch your tone, Loifno. I'd rather not invite the entire realm to gawk," I growl. The idiot really doesn't know the meaning of the phrase. He is a loud fucker.

He throws his head back as he lets out an overly obnoxious laugh. Like I just told him to be as loud as possible and not the opposite.

"Oh, Ciarán. My friend. You still have got it." He pats me on the shoulder, and I roll my eyes. He may be annoying at times, but he is still somewhat trustworthy. I know he wouldn't hurt me or Anna, especially since he owes me a favor.

I loosen my grip on her, and she turns around to face him. Down here, it is more common to stay in our demon form or some semblance of it. I am keeping mine in check since his carnal desire for Anna is so strong, it makes it harder to allow him out.

Loifno is currently half-shifted. He wears pants and no shirt, showing off the blue and purple swirls that curl down his chest and arms. He has no horns, but when he needs them, his fingers can shift into long, needle-like claws.

"Anna, this is Loifno. A friend."

"Nice to meet you." She looks at him, her green eyes sweeping over him as she reaches out her hand for him to shake. He gives her a full smile and moves to shake it, but I quickly slap his hand out of the way, growling. He laughs again. Anna looks up at me, furrowing her brows.

"Sorry, Trouble. That's my fault. Loifno is a special demon that you don't want to touch. He's known as a Mazou. They're a type of demon that works on sorting and accepting the souls that come into hell. They can steal a human's soul with just a touch."

"Don't misinform the girl," the bastard with a death wish says. "I'm a high-ranking demon that looks over the sorters. Do you see this?" he points to the intricate blue swirls on his chest.

Anna nods.

"These become more intricate the higher up the food chain we are. I can control my ability and can even seek certain souls." He smirks. "In fact, I can also look into a human's soul or take one without even touching them." His eyes dart over to me, an amused glint in his gaze. I snap my fingers.

Hell chains burst from the ground, aiming for his throat. He quickly moves out of the way, closer to Anna, as if using her as a shield. Rage simmers just below as my demon begs to be let loose. I hold myself back, knowing Loifno is just teasing us, but still can't help the pure anger that burns through me.

"Loifno, *you*–"

"Interesting girl," he says over me.

"What is?" Anna answers him. She doesn't move, but I see her fighting back a smile. Her eyes shift to mine, and I notice the glint of humor in them.

Oh, she is going to get it when we get home. Someone needs to be punished, and I will gladly dole out the type of punishment she gets over what he would get. She must catch my threat, because a flash of desire causes her pupils to dilate. I smirk at my insatiable girl.

"Your soul. It's been… adjusted."

Her lips fall into a frown as she turns to face him. "What do you mean?"

Loifno meets my eye over her head, and I purse my lips. "Was it something I could have done?" I ask, wondering if maybe keeping her in hell has a negative effect on her after all.

He shakes his head. "Maybe. I'd have to examine it fully to see what it is."

"Is that bad?" she asks.

"No, not necessarily. If it's not fixed before you die, you'll just come to someone like me, where we deal with you."

"Deal with me? What does that mean?"

"That's enough." I cut in. "We don't need to be discussing Anna dying because that's something that will not be happening anytime soon. In fact, she has her own killings to do."

Loifno's eyes sparkle at the mention of death. "Oh yes. You are a killer. I can smell the death surrounding you." He inhales deeply and lets out a satisfied sigh that borders on a moan.

This time when I snap my fingers, he's too distract-ed to avoid the chain that wraps tightly around his throat. A loud crack echoes in the park as his head hits the rocks. Without missing a beat, I grab Anna and walk away as his deranged laughter follows us.

"Is he going to be okay?" she asks.

"Don't worry, Kitten! I've got your scent. I'll be looking for you!" he wheezes as he still cackles on the ground.

"Unfortunately yes. He will be okay," I mutter as we leave him suffocating in the park.

I'll remember to release him later.

Maybe.

tonight is the night

TONIGHT IS THE NIGHT I get to kill Robert F. Gilles. My thirtieth kill, and lucky me, there will be a new moon out. The universe is definitely on my side.

My mind is clear, and my body feels alive with the anticipation of the hunt. Today is when my hard work pays off.

He is still at work on the construction site. It is supposed to be a beautiful skyscraper building where the rich can happily live with little to no care in the world. I've studied the plans. It really does look beautiful.

Too bad he won't get to see it finished.

There is a portable locker room with restrooms and showers for the workers to use and store their stuff while they are on shift. It is something that the owner of the building bought for the workers. It's very thoughtful. Not many people thought of their employees to that extent. Luckily for us, it works beautifully for tonight's plan.

The approaching darkness grows dense.

Robert will be using those showers soon. He found out this morning after his workout at the gym that his water was shut off at home, and he is going to need one after the work they put in today. I only feel a speck of guilt for the rest of the building, who will be waterless, but they can all blame him for that.

In the attached breakroom, I watch through the window as he finishes up his dinner and rinses the container in the sink. He packs his things and heads to the showers.

After a few minutes, I hear the spray of water and leave my hiding spot. I head towards the electricity box that is outside of the portable unit. With a gloved hand, I make quick work of cutting off the lights in the building and the work area. This will also cut the camera footage for a short time while the computers restart. I have about twenty minutes of fun before I need to get out of here.

Robert yells and curses in the sudden darkness. I move to the other side of the building. The bathroom door slams open and wet feet slap against the concrete as he heads towards the power box. Once he's close enough, I sneak around to the locker room to grab his things before hiding under the stairs of the raised building. Not too long after, I see his bare legs coming back to finish his shower and get dressed, but that is too bad for him. He needs to stay naked for what's coming.

"What the fuck?" he yells. The door slams open again as he marches out onto the steps. "Who is out here? Colton! Bill! I swear to fuck, you guys are going to fucking get it come tomorrow morning!" Only silence follows as he continues to yell for people who will most likely be the ones to find his dead, mangled body tomorrow morning.

He walks down another couple of steps before he stops. His feet are right in front of me, right where I need him. "Come out! This isn't fucking funny!"

I take out my sharpest blade and swiftly make a cut, severing the large Achilles tendons on both legs. He lets out a screech of pain and falls down onto the cement.

The blood flows freely, puddling around him.I wonder how long the stain will stay there. Evidence of this moment where I made him bleed. Where he cried. Where he begged. I groan in satisfaction, and Robert must hear me.

"W-who is there?" he asks as he wails on the ground, holding his bloody legs. "What d-do you… wa-want?" His speech comes out in a mixture of pants and sobs, and I swear it's like a symphony to me.

"Oh, Robert." I move out from under the stairs and hold my blade up so that the metal catches the meager light from the emergency lights. "I want you. Is it not obvious?" I stalk closer to him, and he lets out a whimper.

"P-pl-please," he sniffles out. "I-I-I don-"

"Shh. It's going to be okay, Robert." I am standing over him now, relishing in the scent of fear, pain, and blood. I crouch down to straddle him, slapping his hands away from where they held on to his bloody legs. He lets me sit over him like that. The trash is always looking for a woman to give him attention, isn't he? I put my ankles over his shins, forcing the severed tendons to stretch more. He lets out another strangled cry.

My legs begin to feel damp as the blood seeps into my pants, and I sigh. "Look at it. Isn't it beautiful?" I ask.

His wide eyes stay trained on me. He doesn't seem to appreciate it. They never appreciate it. Not like me. His eyes dart towards the knife in my hand, and I know he is going to ruin the moment. He isn't going to let me appreciate this the way I want to.

I tsk before swiftly making three deep slashes. One down each arm and across his face, splitting open his mouth, making half of a joker smile. Now he can't use those well-muscled arms or talk.

He lets out a distorted scream as I sit on top of him and watch as more blood pools beneath him. He flails under me until I bring the knife to his throat.

"Do you know why you're here?" I ask him.

He moans in pain but manages to shake his head.

"You hurt women, Robert. Too many of them. And you know what? Nothing even happened to you. Do you think that's fair? Do you think that's right?"

His face pales at the accusation. Or maybe from the blood loss, I'm not too sure.

"I'll answer that for you. It's not fair, but do you know what? That's okay. Do you know why?" I lean closer to him so I can see him better. "Because you are this reason this is happening, Robert. Because you got away with it, you let me have you. You chose to be my next victim, and I couldn't be happier." I pull down my mask so he can see me smile.

Robert starts crying and blubbering, but I can't understand him. It doesn't matter. Nobody cares what a dying scumbag has to say. They only care that he will be dead.

"Does it hurt?" I whisper.

He doesn't answer. He just keeps crying.

"Well, I'm going to take that as a no, but don't worry. I'll make it hurt." Grabbing his head, I tilt it forward until his half-closed eyes can see me. "I want you to know that after today, nobody will miss you. Soon you will be forgotten, and nobody will cry over your loss. They'll cheer. They'll be happy. So just know that your death is about to make many people very happy. Starting with me."

Robert lets out one last wail as I bring my favorite knife down to slice him open.

CIARAN

you have two weeks

I WALK DOWN THE halls of my father's home as I look for him. He wasn't in his office and I am about to have to resort to summoning him to find him. After talking with Loifno yesterday, we need to talk.

Silently moving up the stairs, I barge into his bedroom but find it empty. I move past the room towards his bathroom and find that also empty. I let out a growl. Do I head back downstairs and try his vault?

He better be fucking here or so fucking help me, I will summon his ass. He'll be pissed, but I don't give a shit. Azrael's been so vague about things, and I am tired of it. I need answers. What did he do to Anna? How do I help her? He's the only one who's ever messed with her. It has to be him.

I round another corner and open the door that leads down into the basement. Faint screaming carries up the stairs, and a small knot of worry untangles itself. After getting to the bottom of the steps, I head straight for the center of the room. He has a human chained up, naked, bloody, and beaten.

A shiver from my already tense demon goes through me at the sight.

"Another stray?" I ask my father, clearing my throat. He is at his tool table wiping off some sort of screwed-up makeshift blade that is coated in blood with a rag that is already dripping wet. Nothing gets done, but he doesn't mind.

The Shadow member whimpers as he is left hanging by his arms. By the look of his dislocated shoulders, he has been here for hours.

"Making an example out of this one, actually," Azrael answers. I nod my head in response.

Even though I am the one in charge of dealing with these punishments, the Balor demons don't stop killings or disciplining the members when necessary. There is no switch that turns off the bloodlust or the ache for retribution.

Having no problem with it as the current leader, I allow it. There are hundreds of thousands of members across the world for us to take our pick from. I am glad for the help, especially since I have been recently distracted.

"So you'll send him back?"

"That's the plan, son." Azrael puts the bloody tool down on the table and wipes his hand on the towel. "To what pleasure do I owe this visit?"

"I'm here for answers."

He sighs, turning back to face me. "Of course you are. What part of traditions don't you understand? You know you're already pushing your limits with the girl."

"There's been more deaths. Someone is killing our Shadow members, and she matches the criteria of the other victims. I will not let her be out there unless it is necessary. You know I can't do that."

Azrael gives me a scrutinizing stare. "So who is killing your flock, Ciarán? Have you figured it out?"

"If I knew that, don't you think I would have already dealt with them by now?" I snap.

He shrugs. "I don't know what you'd do."

Anger rises like hot acid as it races through my veins. I try to control it, although not very well. Our people are being targeted like damn sheep. Anna's fucking life is on the line and he's shrugging like he doesn't give two shits.

I know he could help more if he wanted to. I am only one demon. We may be devils, but we aren't all-knowing beings. We have limitations, and there are many things beyond our capabilities. Nothing angers me more than knowing that at this moment.

The feeling is almost mortal.

"Why are you doing this?" I grit out. "Do you want to see me fail? Is that what this is?"

"No, Ciarán. I don't want to see you fail. This is your trial to pass. It's not my job to give you the answers. It's my job to help you grow and succeed on your own."

"Then why are you being such a jackass about it? Would killing you solve all my problems?"

Azrael laughs. "If you feel that is the answer, you are more than welcome to try." He arches a brow at me in a challenge. It wouldn't be easy, but I know I could do it. In this moment, I am so very tempted.

I need to take my anger out on something. My eyes drift over to the passed-out human that is still strung up. My father lets out a warning growl. It is taboo to help kill or torture someone else's soul, and we both know that. Although if I want to piss him off like he is doing to me, here's an opportunity.

I smirk.

"Go upstairs. I'll meet you up there so we can continue this talk," he barks.

Keeping the smile on my face, I do as he says and head to his study. After a few minutes of washing up, he joins me. The evidence of his downstairs activities completely gone.

I blow out a breath and sink into the couch that only days ago I sat with Anna curled in my lap. Remembering how soft and perfect she is helps to ebb away some of the fiery anger, but only enough to not explode.

"Your time is running out. You only have until the full moon after her twenty-first birthday to kill Theodore. Otherwise, your bond and her memories will be gone forever."

"I know," I mutter.

"What's wrong, son? Don't you think you should be working on killing the man that stands in the way of you and your mate? Is there no urgency?"

Closing my eyes, I let my head fall back onto the couch. "Of course, there's fucking urgency. I need Anna more than I need my black heart to continue to beat, but I couldn't trust myself near Theodore." His name alone is like acid, causing me to spit the next words out. "I knew if I watched him or was alone with him, I'd kill him. After all, he made a claim on Anna, and she wasn't his. She's *mine*."

Azrael makes a noise of empathy, as if understanding what I feel. "Well, I guess it's time for that to be set aside. You must find a good reason to get rid of him, and your time is running out. Shepherds don't make waste of their sheep unless for good reason. You have two weeks before your deadline."

I open my eyes to find him staring back at me. Even though he wears a mask of indifference, his eyes hold a softness to them.

"Okay. After tonight's meeting, I'll start. Even though that means I'll be away from Anna and borderline spending time with the asshole," I grumble.

"That's the spirit, Ciarán. Now, don't you have a meeting to attend?"

"Yeah. Sure do."

I bite back my smile, knowing at least I'll get to see her. Plus, there is the matter of us celebrating her big kill tonight. It is going to be a long night, but it is now or never.

i'm being hunted

Twenty minutes isn't long enough.

I wish I had more time to spend with Robert. I love the feeling of my blade slicing into his firm flesh. Unfortunately, the cuts have to be shallow, and he has to stay in pretty much one piece.

Was it so wrong for me to want to have more fun with him?

It's not my usual piece of art, but I hope the women he hurt still appreciate my work. One less shitbag in the world.

Since my clothes are completely soaked in Robert's blood, they are now wrapped tightly in plastic along with my shoes. I have a new, clean set of gloves and my undergarments on while I hurry to finish the rest of my plan before the cameras turn back on.

There's eight minutes left to make this look like an accident, erase all evidence of me, and leave. I can get dressed when I'm back in the densely wooded area.

Jogging towards the closest front loader truck, I hastily jump in and turn it on. The beast rumbles to life, and I put it in drive as I head straight towards the bloody mess that is Robert F. Gilles. A minute later, the truck thuds as the giant tires run over his body , crushing and popping bones and skin. It is just like popping open a bag of fresh chips.

I put the machine into park, jump out and grab the chain from my bag- one that I had stolen from the site a few weeks ago- and tangle it around the mangled mess of Robert scum.

He hadn't been completely dead when I had left him earlier, but he stopped crying and moaning. Only wheezing and occasional groans were uttered faintly. I didn't want his death to be easy and swift.

No. Robert doesn't deserve that. He needs to experience the pain and humiliation.

Careful to avoid the smeared puddle of blood, I step over him to watch his chest and am satisfied when I see the subtlest of movements. At this stage, he is pretty much dead. The lungs and heart would stop working soon.

His body just doesn't know when to give up. I guess constantly working out has some merit in the end… for me.

Smiling, I hook the chain onto the bottom of the truck and wrap the rest around him, making sure I tangle it around his head. I dig in his bag until I find his headphones, put one in his ear and dropped the other next to him. I then put the truck in neutral and watch as it hitches forward thanks to the slope we are on.

Four minutes are left.

Grabbing Robert's bag, I cut one strap and drop it on the stairs, spilling the contents to make it look like it was likely something he could have tripped over in the dark. How unlucky.

Then he couldn't have heard the truck coming because he had headphones in. What a tragic accident, really. A series of unfortunate events, just one right after another.

I go back to my hiding spot and watch the rest of the show.

The truck is moving slowly, but the chain is now almost taut enough to start dragging Robert. I am excited to see what piece of art his blood creates on the pavement.

I can't wait to share this moment with Ciarán. Knowing he'll be excited just because I am makes warmth bubble in my chest. Just thinking about being with him and the life we will have together, I could just die of happiness.

There is so much that has happened and that I have left to learn, but I know I want to be with him. I know that there is no other man who would be so devoted and accepting of me. I can't deny the connection I feel to him and know that it is only going to grow over time.

Ciarán set my soul on fire and scorched me from the inside out. There is nothing I can hide from him and nothing I want to hide. I want everything with him.

The dragging of the chains reaches a crescendo, and I look up right as they snap and begin pulling Robert across the way. Inch by painful inch. It is too dark to see much, but if I concentrate, the sounds of his bones and flesh moving across the rough pavement can still be heard over the sounds of the machine that parades him away.

There are only seconds left before the power turns back on. Time for me to go.

In the Death Shadow Society, we have rules to follow. One of them being not to play with your kill. Another is not to watch your prey for too long. It's easy to get caught up in watching your masterpiece, but those two rules helped keep us safe and protect us from getting caught.

Whether I want to or not, I have to follow the rules.

It is fine, since tonight I have an excuse to leave. We have a meeting, which means I'll be seeing Ciarán soon.

It's been a while since I have seen anyone. I wonder if they have been looking for me. What did Teddy tell them?

Thinking about that headache puts a damper on my post-kill excitement, so I decide to push those thoughts away.

With a lightness to my movements, I stand up and head out the way I came. The way with no cameras watching me and where the shadows will welcome me with open arms.

I walk back into the treeline that surrounds the construction site. When I'm almost a hundred feet in, unease brushes across my spine. I instantly spin around and search my surroundings, but only darkness greets me. The construction lights flicker on, but it only worsens the surrounding visibility.

I am being followed, but that doesn't feel right. I sniff the air, hoping to catch a hint of the smoky scent I've grown so fond of, but can only smell the surrounding forest mixed with… something clean?

No. It couldn't be.

Instinctively, my fingers brush against my ring finger, but find it bare. My precious gift from Ciarán is in my bag. Shit. I'm going to have to look down to search for it. I just need the ring, then I can be back with him. Back to safety.

Movement on my right causes me to falter. I reach for my knife on instinct. I stay crouched as my eyes scan the area, looking for what is out here with me. It can't be an animal. The movement belongs to something bigger.

Then a blaring alarm goes off in my mind as realization hits me- I'm being hunted.

My breaths come in shallow spurts as panic tries to claw its way down my spine. Fear spreading to my limbs to immobilize me. Gritting my teeth, I force myself to move. I drop my knife and dive for my bag. My hand brushes against the pocket that my ring is in and I quickly pull it out.

I reach to pick up the knife, needing it to cut my hand and to smear my blood on the ring. But I never get to touch it.

An arm bands around me, picking me right off the floor. Before I can do anything else, a cloth goes over my mouth and nose. I try to hold my breath and kick my legs back into their legs and throw back my elbow, but my attacker easily blocks me as he presses the cloth harder to my face.

I choke as my lungs burn for air. A whimper escapes me as I take a deep breath. The last thing I see is the glint of my ring on the ground.

another missing person

One final meeting stands between me and having Anna's body underneath me. I can't wait to see her tonight.

I've only seen her post-kill high from afar, but getting to experience it up close? To see her glow from the thrill of taking another life? What an experience I have waiting for me tonight.

The Crimson Carnival I am currently at is one almost another state away from her meeting.

Just two more hours.

I am using this time to not only fantasize about what my girl and I will do tonight but to mentally prepare myself for watching Theodore Henry. This will really test my resolve to not lay a hand on him unless he deserves it. If he does, then the punishment he will get is *my* choice.

Maybe waiting this long to kill him will be worth it? This must be how my little killers feel after having to do research into and learning habits of their next victims. Us Balor demons have no reason to wait. What we want, we get. When we see a problem, it is swiftly dealt with, and then that is that.

This is part of the problem I have with Anna. The amount of control and restraint that I hold myself to for her is unheard of for a demon, but I do it for her.

It is rare for a demon to be paired with a human. When species mix, it becomes complicated. That is why Anna had to have her memories of me taken away. It was hard when I was younger to accept that. Anna obviously couldn't tell people she was matched with a demon, and now look at the complications it leaves us with.

It took a few years for me to understand. Because of that, I hadn't been allowed outside of Hell until I could control myself enough to not interact with her.

She is worth it, of course. Anna will always be worth it. To me, she is perfection embodied.

So for her, I will be strong and do what needs to be done. For her, I will be a little more patient and rein in my self-control enough to kill her fake fiancé the right away.

Demons who stray from our traditions and pacts are killed in such horrible ways. Since we have no souls, we cease to exist once we feel our years of torturing has come to an end. After getting this close to Anna, I will not throw this opportunity away.

"Unfortunately, it's been a week since she's been heard from. As far as we know, there was no mention of her leaving willingly. She was a loyal follower to our lords after all, but has missed her check-in that was scheduled a couple of days ago."

With that statement, my one track mind shatters as I zero in on the leader of this company.

Another missing person? The killer is becoming more confident and amping up for something. The increasing frequency could mean there is a trigger that set them off for whatever reason.

An itch grows beneath my skin. I need to hurry up this damn thing with Theodore and take care of this problem now.

I am out of time.

"After reaching out to other companies, I've learned that this has become a bit of a trend. It's looking like someone is definitely targeting our younger members. Multiple unpaired twenty-one-year-olds have now been taken. We aren't sure how, but be vigilant."

Murmurs break out across the company, talking about what it could mean that these little wolves in sheepskin are being targeted. It's fine. Soon the killer will make a mistake in front of me and I will catch them. There will be hell to pay, and that will be one less thing to worry about.

"It looks like there are no other correlations between the victims, unfortunately. They were different races, and even though two of them were female and one was male. No other conclusions or reasoning is being drawn at this time, but we are officially issuing a warning to all companies.

"This is no coincidence. We have a rogue killer in our midst, and when they are caught, we will happily turn them over to our demon lords and let them dole out the punishment they deserve. There's a reason that we do not allow ourselves to hunt other killers. That is selfish. We are put here and meant to only serve *them*. Don't forget that. These kills aren't for our benefit. We are just lucky enough to be chosen to serve."

Pride swells through me at the speech. Sometimes the humans are so convincing. Their emotions are so fascinating. How they captivate others with only a few words. If my heart isn't solely focused on growing my power and Anna, I might have actually had some capacity to feel moved.

"It's almost embarrassing to say that we are killers, and yet here we are, being picked off one by one. You know how to summon the lords. If someone is attacking you and you aren't able to subdue them, let that be your last resort. Of course, if the killer is one of us, they would also know how to stop you, so just use your best judgement. We are proud people. Act like it."

I couldn't have said it better myself. Maybe it is time to reward these leaders. Then again, they are just doing their jobs, so maybe not. The only thing they'll find from me is pain when they fail their jobs.

"Now we will show you a picture of Nicole, in case you don't recognize the name. Keep an eye out for her and, more importantly, watch out for yourself."

The leader messes around with the projector contraption, and I decide to take a peek. When I send the Hellhounds to recover the body, it'll be easier to identify them.

I transport myself to the top of the stands in the tent. Not many people are where I stand, waiting alone while I wait for the picture to appear.

A girl pops up. She's what someone would call good looking. Angular features paired with cool eyes and a smirk, as if she knows some joke we don't. Joke is on her. She is dead. She had long, straight blonde hair pulled back into a ponytail.

There is something familiar about her… Nicole was her name? Where have I heard that name before?

Realization jolts me like a sudden splash of icy water. Anna's party.

She was Theodore Henry's secret girlfriend.

my fate

I GROAN AS I turn over onto my side. My head pounds and my dry mouth tastes like shit.

What happened? My brain struggles for a few moments, but a shooting, blinding pain through my skull has me giving up before making too much effort.

Fuck, I'm thirsty. I crack open one eye and find the room is dark. There's a glass of water on the table, and I chug the whole thing before gingerly laying back onto the bed.

Everything is spinning. I am not sure if I need to sit or lie down, but after trying both, I realize nothing makes it better.

The urge to throw up simmers at the surface. I need to find somewhere to do that. I try focusing on my surroundings to look for a trash can or a restroom. An open door across from me looks promising. Stumbling on my feet, I move towards it and am relieved to find the latter.

After purging my stomach contents, I rinse my mouth out in the sink before taking a big gulp of water straight from the faucet. I turn it off and wipe my face with the back of my hand. Catching my reflection in the mirror, I stop to pause. Something is wrong.

My brain tries to process what is happening. Looking down at my hands, I stare until I realize my ring is missing. Ciarán gave me that ring. It's special.

Ciarán. Where is he?

Wait. Where am I?

The nausea in my gut swirls with unease, tempting me to throw up again. Too bad there's nothing left to purge. I look back in the mirror and see I am only in my underwear and bra. If I were with Ciarán, I'd be naked.

If I were alone, I'd be in my tank top and underwear. So what's with my outfit?

Still feeling disoriented, I walk back into the small room and look for a light to turn on. I can't see any damn thing with it being so dark. There is a window, but only darkness bleeds in from outside.

After fumbling around, I finally find the switch. I'm about to flip it when a large hand wraps around mine. I let out a scream before another hand comes down over my mouth. The hand circling around my wrist pulls until both our arms are around me and lifts me off the ground, walking us back into the room.

I'm thrown onto the bed. The motion is horrifying for my body, and I fight back a wave of nausea that hits me. I squeeze my eyes shut as I try to steady myself. The decision leaves me immobilized as a large body lies over me and my hands are pulled over my head.

"Oh, Anna. What's happened to you?" a deep voice purrs.

"Teddy?" I gasp. My eyes fly open as I find a familiar pair of blue eyes glaring down at me. Testing the grip he has on me, I find no give. I won't be leaving unless he lets me.

"That's right, *wife*. Did you think you could just run away from me and humiliate me like that? What kind of woman runs away from her husband?" His free hand goes around my throat. His thumb strokes my jaw as he tilts my head back, forcing me to look up at him.

I scoff. "Don't act so upset. You didn't want me. I don't know why you're acting like you actually care that I left."

His thumb runs over my lips, his eyes zeroing in on them. They flick back up, and I see a glint of pure, cold, seething fury.

I suck in a breath. He can't hurt me. That isn't allowed. But even as I think that, the sneer on his face promises to prove me wrong. My instincts scream at me to escape or fight.

Unfortunately, I am fucked. There is no way I am getting out of here in my condition. Teddy is already bigger and stronger than me. He also hadn't just been drugged.

He leans closer to me until he's less than a breath away from my face. "Do you think I'm not upset?" He whispers against my lips.

I swallow, trying to turn my head away, but his grip on me tightens. "I don't know what to think, Theodore. Just what is it you think you're doing?"

He turns my head sharply, causing another pathetic whimper to slip from my lips. I close my eyes as nausea rolls through me in a brutal wave. He groans in response, grinding his body against me before he drops his face to my neck.

"What I'm doing is wondering why I was missing out on this for so long. That sound. That look on your face is a fucking siren's call. Be weak for me, Anna. Let me have you," he whispers, dragging his teeth over my neck, and I fight another wave of nausea.

Anger sparks inside me, giving me some strength. I try to move, but his hand tightens painfully around my neck. Hot tears burn behind my eyes. I fucking hate Theodore Henry.

"Teddy-" My snarl comes out as a strangled groan he cuts short.

"Do not upset me, Anna. You understand me? I am your husband. You will let me do as I please with you."

"No," I grit out. "I don't want *you*. You chose some-one else? Well, so did I."

Teddy's body goes rigid. "What did you just say?" His lust turns back to the anger that I am so used to seeing on him, but I don't care. Theodore can't have me. I am not his to take.

"I'm. Not. Fucking. Yours."

"You will only be mine. I promise you'll never be anyone else's. I won't allow it."

"Fuck you, Theodore. I'd rather die than be anything of yours."

He glowers. "You're going to regret spewing those words out of that mouth of yours, Anna," he whispers.

"The only thing I regret is not telling you sooner and wasting my life planning to be with you."

Teddy's anger boils over as he pushes me further into the bed until I can't breathe. I try to fight him, but my body is useless. His gaze is filled with acridity as he watches me gasp and struggle for the breath he wasn't going to let me have.

The last thing I see are those crystal blue eyes before the lack of oxygen causes me to pass out for the second time tonight.

CIARAN

fuck these rules

Of course, it had to be Theodore. He got away with this for so long because I had been avoiding him.

Satisfaction swells through me now that I have an acceptable reason to kill him. Tonight is looking better and better. Maybe my father was onto something after all?

I stand outside the Crimson Carnival's infamous tent, waiting for Anna to tell her the good news. My body buzzes with anticipation. She'll be coming to the meeting soon enough. They are mandatory for all to attend. To not show is just inviting me over to remind you why my word is law above all else. There's always a few hundred carnivals going on at once across different countries, though the meetings are staggered so we can regularly monitor them.

I came as soon as the previous meeting was done and now stand surrounded by the familiar smell of popcorn and greased metal. Thinking back to the first time Anna and I met and how sweet her little screams were when we rode those rides years ago.

Once Theodore is dealt with, she will get her memories restored as well as our crystal mating bond. We will do it here, where we first met twelve years ago. It'll be such a perfect moment for us. I can't wait.

The meeting time approaches and the crowd of people coming in is dwindling. I have already seen the Henry's and the Wilson's familiar masked faces go into the tent, but neither Anna nor Theodore have walked past me.

No. He wouldn't have.

Tonight is supposed to be a celebratory night. It's just a coincidence that they're both not here yet.

My false comforting words do nothing to soothe the worry that takes root in my gut. Did she get caught up in her last kill and hadn't realized she is late? If so, I can just take her home and hand out a punishment before making her swear to never leave my side again.

As for Theodore? Hopefully, he had just gotten hit by a bus or something else moronic. Just as long as it doesn't involve Anna.

My worrying festers into anxiety bordering on anger. This is wrong. I teleport back to my seat and scan the faces of the audience one by one, and am devastated when theirs are still not there.

The speaker of the company gets the attention of the crowd as they hush to listen to what the woman has to say. I can't focus on her. She doesn't matter. What matters to me is that I am running out of time to do something about my missing girl and that fucker, Theodore Henry.

I am conflicted.

The meeting is going on, and it will be hours before I can leave. Possibly longer if there is more to discuss. I am supposed to be here for this, but I know that this is time Anna doesn't have to spare. I don't even know how long she has been missing.

Taking a deep breath, I blow it out as I try to calm myself down. I have to think rationally.

Anna is literally a trained killer. She can take care of herself. She has training.

But so does Theodore. He knows everything that she knows. He knows how to stop her, and he is so much bigger than her. This is what makes him such a threat. This is part of why hunting the other killers is forbidden.

It is unheard of for a Balor demon to leave their post. But what am I to do? The woman who is the very air in my lungs is missing. I will suffocate without her.

Can I live without her? Without her even knowing the depth of our bond? Before us even beginning?

No. I can't.

I reach for my necklace that's hidden under my shirt. It is the other half of the stone that links Anna's ring to me. I elongate my fangs, cut my palm open and grab the necklace. I watch as the blood drops onto the crystal and then I am swirling away to where she is.

I show up in a densely wooded area I don't recognize. My eyes scan the area, but I see nobody.

Where am I? Where the fuck is Anna?

No. Please tell me it's not...

I look around on the damp ground for a moment and see the familiar glint of the black stone on the ground. I let out a roar of frustration as my anger calls to my demon. He rips from my skin, and I let him.

I go to the nearest tree and punch it until the bark cracks underneath my knuckles, and even then keep going. The tree groans before it splinters and sways, falling away from me.

He took her. He fucking took her and the one thing that links her to me, that would've taken me to her directly, is in my damned hands and not on her finger!

I let out another roar as I pace the area, trying to rein in my anger unsuccessfully.

Fuck these rules. I should have killed him years ago. Even if it would've lost me Anna, she wouldn't be at his mercy. She would've been safe.

Why was I such a selfish asshole? Why did I wait so long? I was just so focused on what I wanted and didn't have...

I need to just calm the fuck down and think.

Where would he have taken her? I haven't even started watching him yet. I have no idea what his habits are or what property he owns.

But I don't need that.

Realization dawns on me as I put my fingers in my mouth and blow out a harsh whistle. Soon the familiar sound of baying approaches, accompanied by the thundering of paws. Before I know it, three hellhounds stand ready before me.

"I need you to find Anna Wilson right now. Do NOT touch her. Lead me to her." I hold out my hand with her ring, and they sniff it before sniffing the air for a moment.

Toil barks out a second later and begins running towards an invisible scent he caught on to. The others follow him, and so do I.

Hold on, baby. I promise I'm coming for you. Just please be okay.

as dead as a doornail

MY THROAT IS SORE and throbbing, but at least I don't feel nauseous when I wake again. The head fog and dizziness seem to have dissipated, but from where Teddy's hand was, I'm sure is seriously bruised.

I move my hand to prod the tender spot, but am confused when I find my wrists tightly restrained.

The sound of metal on metal rings through the room, startling me. I move my head to find my wrists now handcuffed to the bedframe. My hands are severely pale and- now I realize- painfully numb since the circulation has been cut off to them for who knows how long. I shift as if to scoot up on the bed, only to find my feet also cuffed to the bottom of the bed.

My eyes dart around the room. It's still dark, but I can see that Teddy isn't in the room with me this time.

I glance at the cuffs on my wrists and test my mobility. It's intense and painful, but I push past it.

This is something I can get out of. Something I can handle. I begin dislocating my thumb when the door swings open, slamming against the wall. Startled, I jump.

Teddy stalks into the room. He stares at me for a moment, and I glare back. I am stronger now. If he wants to play with me, I am going to give him hell.

Something glints in his hands, and my eyes flick down to find him holding a knife. My breath catches slightly before I look up and see the smile on his face.

"What's wrong, Anna? Don't you like knives?"

I don't take the bait.

"You've messed up. You made a mistake." I tell him, keeping my voice even and low.

"A mistake? What could that be, hmm?"

"We have a meeting tonight. You know we aren't allowed to miss those."

"I'll gladly take those consequences. I wouldn't miss this moment for the world." Teddy smiles down at me and steps closer until he reaches the foot of the bed.

I keep my gaze steady as I watch him.

"Tell me, Anna. Was that trash that you left me for worth it? You see where choosing him over me has left you? It's not too late to change your mind. There will be a training period, of course, and I know you're a slow learner, but I think that's what will make it fun."

I scoff. "Oh yeah? And what would *Nicole* think about that?"

"Who?"

I roll my eyes. "The pretty blonde you brought to my birthday party as your date?"

He frowns before realization dawns. "Oh! Nicole. It's hard to care about what a dead woman would think."

I blink up at him. "She's... dead?"

"As dead as a doornail."

"You..." I let my unfinished question trail off. A knot forms in my gut.

Teddy smiles at me before getting on the bed and straddling me. "Me," he answers.

I pull at my restraints out of instinct, but it only causes a deep ache to shoot through my limbs. I am not going to leave this bed alive.

He drags the blade over my legs lightly. Goosebumps break out over my skin as a bead of sweat rolls down my head, falling onto the bed. My breaths come in shallow, quick pants as the knot in my gut seems to sink.

"You can get into a lot of trouble for that, you know." My voice comes out as a whisper, but it feels so loud in this room.

He shrugs.

"And me? My family will look for me." I am trying to use logic to get him to come to his senses. Knowing that is easier to appeal to than empathy.

His smile grows. "Actually, you see, that's the best part. You ran away. Nobody knows where you went, and nobody has gotten in contact with you for weeks. With all the other missing Shadows, it would just make sense to add you to the list."

"Missing… Shadows? What are you talking about?" The sinking feeling shoots through my chest, settling at the base of my tender throat and making it hard to swallow.

Teddy lets out a dramatic sigh. "It's no surprise I have been having trouble with the idea of being married to you. Ever since you were a little brat, I knew you'd only cause me headaches, and I didn't want to be associated with you. A year ago I realized how little time I had left until you trapped me. I became agitated. I was already dating other people, pretending you weren't about to end my life, but one day I had to face reality. You were going to take away my freedom, and that thought made me so angry I just snapped."

My breath comes faster. bI am trapped and at the mercy of my ex-fiancée. How did this happen? My life is just getting started.

"Jenny was her name- my first kill. She did nothing wrong, but one night I acted on my anger and took it out on her. The high I felt after that kill was unlike anything I had ever experienced before. She was a Shadow after all, someone who could've stopped me, yet she couldn't. I was better."

I can't believe what he is saying. Him telling me doesn't mean anything good for me. Teddy continues to drag the knife across my skin, but is now applying more pressure.

"Then there was Peter. I wanted to see if I could get away with killing a man. Someone physically on my level. Being with him did make me feel things I was surprised to feel. Maybe I had liked him more than I thought, but my desire to kill him was stronger." He shrugs.

"And lastly, Nicole." He finally breaks the skin, and I let out a small hiss as he presses further, slicing deeper. The wounds are still shallow, and his movements are slow and languid, making them more painful. I bite back a cry, but soon my muscles begin to shake from the pain. "On paper, you could say she was the best when it came to skills and such, but when her petty emotions caused her to attack you, I had to get rid of her."

There's a long pause as he focuses on his blade work

When most of my abdomen is covered in weeping red scores, his knife moves up to my chest. Finally, a scream emerges from my throat as the pain becomes unbearable.

"Mmmm. I love that sound," Teddy murmurs. "I'm glad I got rid of her, you know. When I saw you leave with someone else when you were supposed to be mine, that's what made me realize I had to keep you. That you are meant for me and only me. I have taken you for granted, but I won't be making that mistake twice."

My body jerks against the restraints, as my natural instincts scream at me to fight him off. His knife is at my throat now. Tears stream down my face, blurring most of him, but I can still see his crystal clear blue eyes staring down at me.

"I'm almost sorry I have to punish you like this. Your body is so perfect. It was mine long before it was his. Now you will forever be mine. My wife. My favorite kill. You don't know how happy I am that I get to own these last few moments with you. You understand how precious they are."

Then he slices across my throat, this time quickly. It's not as painful as the rest of the cuts. The only pain I really feel is anguish as my vision darkens.

Teddy leans over me as if to kiss me. Blood spills out of my mouth and down my chin. An inch a way his hot breath brushes against my lips "Good bye, Anna. I'll always love you."

He suddenly disappears. A moment later, a dark, horned figure replaces him.

Ciarán.

His face is a mixture of pain and anger. I reach out a hand and feel a sense of relief as I get to touch him, for the last time. At least the last face I see is his. My breaths are labored as they rattle through my chest, failing to escape my severed trachea.

Something clicks into place as a burning warmth of emotions rushes through me. Emotions pulsating, and I realize they're a mixture of Ciarán's and mine.

It's our bond. We are mated together.

He pulls me into his chest and cradles me gently.

Please don't leave me, Anna. You're not fucking allowed to. I can't exist without you. Please. Ciarán's thoughts are like a warm embrace swirling in my mind. Even if they crack open my heart to hear his begging. I am fortunate that I get to hear him one last time.

A final breath passes painfully from my lips as I stare into his hauntingly beautiful gray eyes.

I wish I had more time to love you. Is my final thought to him before I die.

wiped off the map

My whole fucking world burns to ash as I hold Anna's lifeless body in my arms.

Her once radiant green eyes stare blankly at me. Tears that had streamed from them, stain her beautiful face. They mix with her blood that still drips from her lips and throat.

I hold her to me, never wanting to let her go. Regretting that I ever had. Regretting that I ignored Theodore

Henry for so long and letting him murder the very core of my being. The woman who is branded on my bones.

A microscope of consolation is our bond locking into place after I split Theodore in two. She felt the depth of love I had for her. She understood the carnage that would be left in her wake.

I felt her love burning for me. Even if I finally got to feel whole with her bond colliding with mine for that one second, it is never going to be enough. My very being wants and demands more, and now I'll never have that. I lost everything.

My body releases a wave of power, and hell flames erupt on the edges of my vision, consuming the house before spreading out swiftly. Theodore's lifeless body erupts in flames first. I had ripped him in half, using up quite a bit of my power. His legs and most of his left side of his body catching fire before his head and what's left of the right side. I didn't get to enjoy killing him, but that doesn't matter because I was too late. Anna is still dead, and it's all my fault.

Her face continues to pale, and I finally allow myself to look away as I tilt my head back and let out a strangled roar. I scream and scream until my throat is raw and I'm surrounded by glass and flames.

My gaze lingers on my perfect mate's now mutilated body. Dozens of cuts and slashes are all over her, staining her olive skin red. The hellfire burns hotter and draws closer to us. I hold Anna tighter as I bury my face in her hair and cry.

I am ready to follow Anna into death because nothing will ever hold meaning for me. I don't care what happens next, and am devastated to know there even is life without her.

I'll burn in agony for hours before I'd allow myself to die. Anna's body will be long destroyed by then, but it's fine. I don't deserve to hold her or even look at her in my final moments after what I have done.

The flames are only inches away, and a wave of sadness hits me as Anna's hair singes from the heat. I give her one final kiss as the flames lick my skin and searing pain burns through me.

In the next heartbeat, I'm back in Hell. The familiar, tainted air surrounds me. My gaze shoots up to find the reason for why that is.

"Aren't you a dramatic fucker?" Loifno says with a smirk on his smug face.

My arms feel lighter, and I glance down to find Anna is no longer with me. My head snaps up, and I snarl as I lunge at him. His grin widens as I tackle him to the ground. "Where the fuck is she?! What did you fucking do with her?!" I roar as I let my fists fly.

He laughs as I throw punch after punch into his face. After a few seconds, he grabs me and throws me off him.

"Bring her back!" I yell.

He jumps up, and I lunge at him again.

"Calm the fuck down. Wasn't destroying that town enough? Just how much power are you holding in there?"

I pause. "What?"

"Your flames. They spread so quickly that they set the whole town on fire, since it is a dry season." Loifno shrugs. "The whole place is gone. Wiped off the map."

For a moment, I am worried about Azrael's reaction before I remember I had been in the middle of killing myself. I scowl at Loifno. "Why didn't you let me die?"

He grins again, and I hold back my urge to lunge at him, but only barely so.

"Don't you remember I owe you a favor?"

I growl. "And you think that not letting me die is you repaying that favor? Because if so, you are sorely mistaken, Loifno."

"No, my surprise is better than that. Although maybe this means you owe me two favors now? So maybe you should treat me better? Although I do like this rough side of y-"

"Get to the fucking point."

"Fine. Of course you'd ruin my surprise," he grumbles. "Close your damn eyes."

I narrow them instead. "I'm not playing these fuc-"

"Do it!" The demon side of him wins out as his anger flares. All pretense of amusement gone. I eye him a moment longer before doing as he asks and closing my eyes.

"Search for your bond," he snaps.

I'm about to kill the fucker for playing games with me when I realize I feel her. My eyes fly open. "She's... She... How?"

His easy-going demeanor slides back with that smug smirk and I swear I could fucking kiss the cocky bastard.

I don't care. She is alive, and he has something to do with it.

"Apparently you've been feeding her your blood, which caused her soul to come to me as it had registered that you were the one who was dead, which made no sense. When I realized it was her, I was shocked. The idea came to me then, since she was already transitioning, and I turned her, sort of."

"What does that mean? What did you do?" I can't believe this. I crowded closer to him, and my hands ached with the grip I had on his shoulders.

"It'll be easier to show you. Come on, she's waiting for you."

Without a second to waste, he transports us to the Gates of Hell, where a steady stream of souls are pouring in. We scan in at the gates and are allowed to pass through.

Since souls are so precious here, they literally fuel Hell, it's the only place with actual security. Any and all kind of teleporting is banned beyond these gates. If you try to, you just end up back at the gate.

My skin is crawling with anticipation as we walk through the processing and sorting areas until we are up in the high chambers. It's where peculiar souls- souls with a deal in process or tied to them, or severely damaged souls- go. This is where the overseers like Loifno reside and work.

Finally, we get to Loifno's area, and he opens the door for me. I eagerly rush into the room, letting my bond guide me forward. I get to another door and slam it open to find who I'm looking for.

"Hey there, devil boy," a voice as sweet as honey carries over to me. I quickly find those beautiful, bright green eyes and choke on air. "Miss me?"

speak of the devil

DARKNESS SWIRLS WITHIN ME. It unfurls and expands, consuming every inch of the old Anna and turns her into something different. Something strange.

Heat spreads throughout my body with that darkness. Everything burns. Then there's a spark of something else. I follow that spark and get a glimpse of what has been locked away.

Moving forward, I unlock the memories, and flashes of the past come at me. A younger Ciarán staring down at me while I wait to be introduced to my mate. Me trying to make him laugh. Hearing his voice for the first time. Him cheering me up. Us holding hands as we rode the rides in the empty park at the Crimson Carnival.

Then his father, Azrael, whom I had met before. Ciarán looking scared and angry and then excited.

We were mated, but Teddy had to be used as a cover. Then my memories were stolen.

Ciarán and I being paired. We were meant to be together. That explains why I could feel him, why we heard each other when I..

When I...

My eyes snap open, and I gasp, inhaling a lungful of air.

"There she is! You gave me quite a fucking scare there," Loifno exclaims.

I look up and see him looking down at me.

"What happened? I thought I was..." My hand trails up to my neck where I feel a scar running across it.

"Dead? Oh yeah. You were pretty dead." He laughs.

My brows pinch together, but something feels different. I raise my hand to inspect the change on my head, but Loifno's strong hands stop me before I can. He pins them to the table and gives me a deliberate look. The contrast from his laughter to his strength is unsettling.

"What are you doing?" I ask. The memories of recently being tied down are not making this a very positive moment right now.

"Listen, Kitten. You died. You are in Hell now, at the Gate. This is where all the souls come in. Do you remember Ciarán telling you about the type of demon I was?"

Confused, I let my agitation ebb away as I think back to a few days ago. Or was it weeks? The memory shakes free slowly. Loifno is a Mazou. A soul-taking demon. "Yes," I answer.

"Good. Well, as a higher up, I deal with the flagged or strange souls. Yours was flagged, and I think it's because you were drinking Ciarán's blood. Have you been?"

"Drinking his..." I think back to our heated sexual encounters and realize I have. My face heats and Loifno raises a brow at me. "Um, yes, actually. A few times on accident."

He smirks as if he knows what I was thinking, and my cheeks burn hotter. "Well, demons don't really have souls. Not technically. We do have a life force that stems from our heart. It makes our blood very potent, especially for humans. It caries a type of curse in it, but most people usually don't drink enough to change or not as much in a short amount of time."

"What are you saying?" I am feeling more confused than before he started speaking.

"What I'm *saying* is Ciarán's blood in your body affected your soul and started transforming you. When you died, it flagged you and sent you to me. Since you have a strong bond with him, plus the mixture of your blood and your mating bond in place, I was able to recreate you in a sense and transform you."

"So I'm… a demon?" The words coming out of my mouth are surreal.

"Almost. Since you have your human body back, you'll be transitioning for a while. Unfortunately, I can't heal what had been done, but I was able to manipulate it into something prettier."

I think about the lacerations on my body and the pain I felt when Teddy was carving through my flesh. A shudder rolls through me, and Loifno uses that time to let go of my hands. I peek down at my arms and notice my skin is dark, like Ciarán's, but not all the way black. Red lines that resemble vines branch over my flesh.

Sitting up, I look down at my skin and find the lines run all over my chest and torso.

"What did he do to me?" I mumble.

"No, it's not what he did to you. It's what you do with what he gave you that matters. He's dead, and he's not coming back."

I look back at Loifno. "Ciarán killed him."

He nods and grins at me. "Speak of the devil, I'd better go get him before he does anymore damage."

"Anymore?"

Loifno walks towards the door and turns back to me. "Oh yeah, he burned that town to ashes for you."

I CAN FEEL HIM as he gets closer.

My body has been slowly processing what is happening, but as the minutes tick on, I register more of what

I'm feeling. An echo of an ache in my chest where I feel Ciarán's pain and distress throbs softly in my chest. It slowly shifts to his anticipation and my excitement.

Loifno has told him, and now they are on their way.

I stand in front of the mirror and take in my new appearance. I have horns and fangs similar to Ciarán, but mine are tipped in blood red.

My body is smoky black except for the scars that are there- evidence of how I had been murdered. I stare at the blood-red vines that crawl up to my chest and down my arms, standing out from my demon skin.

At least they were a nice pattern?

Although I am worried about what Ciarán will think. I know I'll figure it out soon, as he is almost here.

The front door to Loifno's residence opens, and then, a second later, the bedroom door slams open as Ciarán bursts through. His anxiety melts into disbelief, and I smile at him.

"Hey there, devil boy. Miss me?" I tease.

"You have no fucking idea, Trouble," he mutters. His eyes burn into me as he stands there. Time stands perfectly still for one heartbeat before he rushes in and pulls me into a bone-crushing hug. Ciarán's face buries into my neck and he deeply inhales.

I sigh, relishing in the feeling of wholeness. At feeling right in this moment and being able to be with him. I put my arms around his neck and pull him closer to me. He tenses for a moment before chuckling.

"You've gotten stronger," he says.

"Have I? I don't really know what I'm doing or anything," I admit sheepishly. I am still in my demon form. Unable to change back since I don't know how.

He pulls back and cups my face. "We will figure it out. Don't worry. I'm just so fucking glad you're alive right now." His gray eyes reflect the depth of that truth, but more than that, the connection between us flares to life. It permeates the air, swallowing me whole and consuming me fully.

Just as I am fully able to understand what we are and what it means to be together, he kisses me. His kiss is searing like he is trying to brand himself to me, and I am going to let him.

alone

She is real. She is fucking real and here with me.

Her scent is different. Spicier than before. Even though she is a demon now, when I look into her sparkling eyes, I still see my girl. Anna.

I hold her in my arms. My lips mold against hers as I try to feel more of her. I need to drown myself in everything that's her. I will cherish her harder, love her deeper and, more importantly, not let her go.

Loifno clears his throat behind me, and I swallow the growl in my throat as I force myself to remember he is the reason she is with me. My shoulders sag forward slightly as I reluctantly pull back.

"I remember you from when we were younger," she says. Anna peers up at me as I look down, studying her face. Her features remain the same. My eyes lingering on her kiss-swollen lips. I tuck a few dark strands of hair behind her ear before letting my hand trace her jaw.

"Yeah?"

"All that time you had to watch. I didn't know," she breathes.

"You were always mine. Of course I'd follow you everywhere."

She smiles, flashing me her teeth that now have two cute little fangs sticking out. They are tipped red, and my breath catches in my throat as I admire them.

"So pretty," I murmur as my fingers lightly press against the sharp tips.

Anna blushes, and I smirk down at her.

"Well then, I'm glad I could bring you two back together. It does warm my heart, really," Loifno says.

"Now I guess it's time I explain how this is going to work."

I turn around, keeping Anna behind me. "How what is going to work?"

"She's not a full demon. She's still transitioning, and when she's done, she will be something entirely different. Look at her markings. That's what gives her away."

Anna moves next to me, and my gaze roams over her. She has red markings spreading all over her body that are varying shades of red.

"You said you made them this way," Anna says.

"Technically, I did. But they are actually the telltale markings of another creature. Have you heard of a Hellspawn?"

"The name is familiar," I answer.

Loifno grins. His gaze slides over to Anna, and I pull her closer to me. "They are rare. Few can withstand the change, and the conditions aren't always right. There's never any guarantee one will turn out correctly."

"What does this have to do with her?"

"I'd say everything, considering that's exactly what she is. Well, a type of one. She's what's known as a Bloodshade. Part demon, part bloodsucker."

My body goes rigid.

"A bloodsucker?" Anna asks.

Loifno nods excitedly. "You, Kitten, are one in a million. Your drive and bloodlust helped to create you."

"But I'll be drinking… blood?"

"You're focusing on just one aspect of it. You're missing the big picture." Loifno's skin ripples as his agitation eats away at his patience.

A warning growl emits from my throat as my demon's aura spreads out in the room. My urge to protect Anna after losing her hours ago surpassing my manners. Loifno only smiles as his body calms in response. I narrow my eyes at him. He is definitely up to something.

"Now, friend. There's no need for the dramatics."

"What the fuck do you want? Just spit it out and tell us," I growl. I should be less hostile towards the demon who saved the one thing that matters in my life, but I can't be bothered to. It doesn't help that I no longer have a debt over his head. In fact, it is I who owes him greatly, and he knows it.

"It's obvious there's a bit of tension here. There's the fact that Anna has gone through a big change and is still transforming. She will need to be coached through it as well as learning how to control herself-"

"I can teach her how to be a damned demon by myself. I think I have that down," I spit out.

"Yeaahh... Except no. While your line is now a part of her, her Bloodshade part needs to be dealt with, and that is something you cannot help with."

My jaw tightens, and I'm about to give the demon a piece of my mind when I feel Anna's hand on my back.

"It's fine. I'd rather learn how to do this correctly." She smiles up at me. "I haven't even learned how to look normal yet."

Loifno laughs. "Oh, Kitten. This is your normal look. Doesn't it feel more natural?"

Anna shrugs.

"Cool it with the *fucking* nicknames already," I mutter. Loifno being the asshole, he is just grins at me.

"You'll get used to it. Now, why don't we get ready to show you your new home?" he purrs.

"What do you mean?" Anna asks.

"Well, you'll be living here, of course."

"The fuck she will!" I snarl. This time, I can't stop myself from lunging forward.

"Absolutely, she will." He holds out his hand to her, his eyes glowing bright. "Anna, take my hand and come with me."

I look behind me to see Anna stiffen up before hesitantly reaching out her hand and taking his. My arm bands around her to keep her next to me. "What are you doing, Loifno? Stop!"

"Be careful, Ciarán. I can just as easily make her forget about you. It'll be trickier, but I can and will do it. Don't make me abuse my power like that," he threatens.

Loifno regards me, but I am fucked, and he knows it. Still holding her, Anna's face tilts up to me. Her eyes are glowing too, but only slightly. She has a small frown on her face, but otherwise looks okay.

"What are you going to do?" I swallow.

"Train her, teach her how to be herself! Use her for one tiny little mission and then she'll be free to go."

"What kind of mission?" As soon as I ask, I regret it. I know I will not like his answer.

"Just to kill a certain someone. Nothing your trained killer can't handle, I assure you."

"Who?"

"You're not going to like the answer…"

"WHO, Loifno?" I need to know.

"Marzikel."

I suck in a breath. A chill shoots through my fiery veins at the name. Marzikel Onos is a ruthless, power hungry demon king. One of the three kings of hell. Nobody crosses him, because nobody can get to him and live. To most demons, he is the boogeyman. "No. You can't do that. You can't send Anna to him."

"It's not your choice. You owe me big, and this is the repayment I'm demanding. I'm even being generous and offering services along with my favor to help her along. Now give her to me, or you can say goodbye to her now and forget ever seeing her again."

"Can't I say good bye to her? Properly?"

He stares at me a long moment before narrowing his eyes. "No."

With that, he wrenches Anna from my grip and holds her to him. I move to lunge at him, a growl in my throat, but he snaps his fingers and I find myself back in my home. Alone.

"NO!"

I let out a roar of pure anger. I throw my fist out at the closest thing to me. Sounds of walls, stone, and glass shattering and cracking as I throw punch after punch, but I'm not satisfied. It doesn't help. Nothing will help until I get Anna back.

He took her, and he is going to regret it.

A Note

Thank you for reading my first story, written by me!

I wrote this as a challenge to write something small, but then I decided to continue. There was an opportunity to end it in one book, but then felt like Anna and Ciarán's story wasn't quite done yet. I thought about just making this book longer, but I still wanted it to be a smaller, quick read. Ya know? Something spooky and sexy. It ended up being a little more horrorble (-a pun) than I thought it'd be.

For those of you who know me in real life, I hope your love for me overpowers your need to judge me (lol).

Anyway, I'm thrilled with how it turned out and hope you love it and look forward to the next part of their story!

About the author

Estella Oscura is a pen name used by Estella to write in the genres that she loves: Dark Romance, Paranormal, Fantasy, Romantasy, or anything spicy.

What she loves the most is letting the characters in her mind come to life so everyone else can enjoy them.

Her day job lets her interact with different and interesting people, which helps inspire her colorful character quirks and dialogue.

When not writing, she is daydreaming about writing.

Follow me on Instagram for updates or to say hi!
@oscura_authors
Subscribe to newsletters and more on
https://estellaoscura.com

Also by

Estella Oscura:

Paranormal Dark Romance, M/F series
Devil's Shadow:
Always Mine

Marissa & Estella Oscura:

COMING SOON
Romantasy, Why Choose series
Realms of the Gods:
Forgotten Beasts